I0547151

CASSIAN

SAVAGE DRAGONS BOOK 3

KATHI S. BARTON

This is a work of fiction. Names, characters, places, and incidents are products of the author's imagination or are used fictitiously and are not to be construed as real. Any resemblance to actual events, locations, organizations, or persons, living or dead, is entirely coincidental.

World Castle Publishing, LLC
Pensacola, Florida

Copyright © 2025 Kathi S. Barton
Hardback ISBN: 9798273819115
Paperback ISBN: 9798891264861
eBook ISBN: 9798891264878
First Edition World Castle Publishing, LLC, November 17, 2025
http://www.worldcastlepublishing.com

Licensing Notes

All rights reserved. No part of this book may be used or reproduced in any manner whatsoever without written permission, except in the case of brief quotations embodied in articles and reviews. No part of this book may be used or reproduced in any manner for the purpose of training artificial intelligence technologies or systems.
Cover: Cover Designs by Karen
Editor: Karen Fuller

Prologue

Raven loved her job. She'd been working in the fast food restaurant for the past five years since turning sixteen and needing some extra cash for a car that she wanted to purchase. Since then, she'd not just gotten her a second or third-hand car, but she'd been promoted to head cashier, too. It paid a little more than she'd been making, and she got to be the one in charge while they were all busy at the cash register.

But today, sadly, was her last day. She was going to finish her college education and become a lawyer. Taking night classes all this time had suited her needs well, but now that she was having to intern and go to classes, it had become a bit too much for her. She'd been able to secure enough grants to not have to work, but she was going to have to pinch her pennies until they screamed for mercy.

"What are you going to do with all your free time?" So many customers thought that she was just quitting so as not to have to work anymore. "I bet you have a list a mile long to do when you're off." "I'm betting that in a month you'll be back like nothing happened." "You're too good a worker not to have a job." Her favorite one, people said to her, was "So you've won the lottery, have you?" She could only wish that the last one was true.

But the people that she worked with knew what she was doing. Not all of them understood her need for higher education, but she didn't care. It had been a dream of hers to be a lawyer since she'd been to her first court hearing at six years old.

Her parents were divorced. And they both wanted her to live with them. Not because they loved her. No, her parents only wanted the child support the other would have to pay. She knew this the day she was seated in the big chair by the judge and asked what her opinion was about living with one or the other of them. She looked at the older man and told him she didn't want to live with either of them, but would very much like to live with her grannie, who had been raising her since she could walk. That threw a big bomb on the way things went after that.

So at age six, she moved in with her grannie permanently, and both parents had to pay the dreaded child support to her mother's mom. They didn't want her anyway, and with them having to pay support, they didn't feel as if they had to visit her either. Fine by her, she loved her grannie very much.

"It's time for your break." She nodded at the assistant manager and grabbed her drink. She got a free meal daily, but had long since gotten tired of the same food daily and brought herself in something to eat now. As she was eating her PB&J, a peanut butter and jelly sandwich, she tried to ignore the man whose office was right next to the breakroom. "You know there's a fat bonus for any one of us who can talk you into staying just where you are. You should think of the people you're leaving behind. They're going to miss you."

"I'm leaving here, not dying. They can visit if they want." The fact was that no one knew where she lived, and she liked that just fine, too. She loved her job and only somewhat liked the people that she worked with. "I'm going to school and I won't have time to work a full-time schedule. Not even a part-time one."

She didn't point out to him either that if she stayed, she wouldn't be leaving anyone behind. Sometimes Daniel didn't think before he spoke, and it made him sound stupid. Or maybe he was. She didn't really care. He kept at her during her break about leaving and the bonus so much that she took the last fifteen minutes of her break outside in the cold.

Her classes started next week, and she was looking forward to studying a bit more. She didn't own a television or even a radio, but she could travel a bit, and she was going to see her grannie and hang out with her for a couple of days. Then she was going to get her apartment in order before everything started happening.

When her break was over, she went back in to clock in and start on the register again. While she'd been gone, they had put someone else on her line, and she decided to clean up the lobby. It was a mess since the kids were off from school today, and it took her an hour to get things back to looking good. One of the other people she worked with said they'd take out the trash, and she was all for that. It had been cold standing out there, and she was glad that she didn't have to go back out.

At the end of her shift, she was standing to clock out when Daniel started harassing her again. It really was getting old the way he kept at her all the time. She thought because she was older than him, it was what made him think that bossing her around was fun, but she just wanted to do her job and go home. He was making it so that she didn't enjoy coming to work as much with him always on her about something.

"Can you stay over?" She told him no, she already had plans. "Just for an hour. I need someone to watch the lobby for me while I run to the bank. It won't be that bad."

"No. I want to go home. You should have asked me before I made plans and clocked out." He followed her out to her car. "Just leave me alone. As of ten minutes ago, I no longer work here. I want to go home."

"Damn it, why do you have to be such a stubborn

bitch all the time about everything? It's just an hour or two. I have to run to the bank, and you can keep an eye on things while I'm gone." She told him that it wasn't her job that he should have gone earlier when there were more people there. "Well, I didn't, did I, and now I'm telling you that you're going to get your ass back in there and wait for me to return. I won't be but a couple of hours, as I have shit I have to do."

"I'm not going back in there." The slap to her face startled her so much that she fell against her car. "What do you think you're doing? You hit me."

"I know what I did, and now you're going to do what I say and get your ass back in there so I can run some errands. I'm sick of you thinking that you're better than anyone else who works here, and now you're going to do what I tell you. I'm your boss." She shook her head, still holding onto her face. When he hit her again, she felt her head hit her car, and the pain was blinding for a second. Just long enough for him to start dragging her by the hair back into the building. This was going too far.

Fighting him to get away from him, she hurt her arm and ribs. The man was tossing her to the cold pavement even as she was trying to catch her breath. He was really hurting her the way he was beating on her, and she knew that she was bleeding from her mouth and nose. There was no telling where else she was bleeding by the time she was inside the building.

"I've called the police." She didn't know who was speaking, but they said that they were recording it too. Daniel didn't seem to mind what they were saying, since she was in the building again, he was leaving. He told her she'd better be there when he returned, too, or he was going to give her worse than he had already. "They're on their way, Raven. I've told them that he's hurting you."

Daniel was going toward the door when he suddenly turned and came back to her. With a punch to her face, she fell backwards and hit the lobby floor. While there, he drew back his leg and kicked her in the ribs. Everything blacked out from that point on.

Waking up, she knew that she was in the emergency room. Moving her body around so that she could see if someone was with her, she cried out in pain. Every part of her body hurt, and she was sure that when she sat up, she was going to be sick too. What had been wrong with him?

"I'm here." She looked in the direction of the voice. "My name is Cassian Savage. I was in the restaurant when you were dragged in."

"He hurt me because he wanted me to stay while he left for a couple of hours." Thinking hurt as well as her jaw, and she asked for something to drink. When she was given a sip of water, she tried to focus on the man in front of her. "I can't make you out. It's like you're a blurry blob."

"Gee, thanks." He laughed, and she decided that he had a good laugh. "Anyway, Daniel was arrested, and your friends turned over the recording of him following you out of the building and to your car. I'm afraid that I arrived too late to stop him from kicking you — you have two broken ribs in addition to other injuries. But he's claiming that since you're his employee, you should have just done what he said, and that wouldn't have had him hurting you. He blamed it all on you."

"Of course he did. He leaves like that every day and is gone for a few hours. No one ever said anything because he usually leaves someone in charge, and it's good to get away from him. Today, he decided that I was going to watch things while he was gone. It's my last day, and I'd already clocked out for good." She wondered why she was telling this man what had happened when all she wanted to do was beg someone for something for the pain. "Who are you again?"

"Cassian Savage. You have a concussion as well. This is the third time we've talked. They said you might have a raging headache, too. Did you want me to call someone for something for pain?"

"Yes, please. I'm sure you have better things to do than to wait around here for me to get meds." He said that he was enjoying himself. "Good for you. I don't know if you know this or not, but it's not terribly romantic to enjoy a woman who is in pain right now."

He laughed again. While she was getting something in her IV, the meds just floated over her. He sat down in the chair again and picked up what she thought was a newspaper. Well, if he wanted to just sit around while she napped, good for him.

The police came to see her a few minutes after she got her pain medication. They asked her to tell them what had happened, and she couldn't believe that Cassian or whoever he was didn't leave. They didn't even make him go. After telling them everything she could remember, Cassian told them that he had knocked Daniel out with his fist, and that was where he was when they had arrived. Flat out on the floor was a good place for her former boss.

"Did he ever hit you before?" She said no, but so far as she knew, no one had ever challenged him before. "And what made you do it this time? Was there something that you said to him or he said to you that set him off?"

"Today was my last day, and because I was leaving, he said something about not getting a bonus that was being offered if someone could get me to stay. I didn't know anything about that until my lunch break, where he insisted that my going to college wasn't as important as him getting the bonus that was there for the taking." The officer asked her if she wanted to press charges. "Yes. There wasn't any reason for him to knock me around like he did so that he could go on break for a couple of hours."

"Does he usually take a two-hour break in the afternoon?" She told them that he did it on her days working, but she didn't know if he did it on her days off. "Has he ever left you in charge before. Or in this case, wanted you to be in charge before?"

"No. I don't want to be in charge. I was head cashier, but I didn't have to do anything but take over the register when someone had a break." The officers asked her again if he'd left her in charge before. "No. Like I said, I don't want to be in charge."

The hospital was going to keep her overnight because of the head injury. By the time she was settled in her room, her manager and the district manager came into her room. She didn't want to keep going over the same questions all the time, but she knew in order for Daniel to get what he deserved, she was the one with the power to put him there. She never liked him anyway.

All the time she was being questioned, Cassian was right there with her. He even, at one point, said that she'd had enough questions for one day and that they'd have to come back tomorrow. She didn't understand why her bosses left when they did, but was kind of glad for it. She really had had enough of the same questions over and over.

"What happens now, do you know?" Cassian told her that Daniel would stay in jail until such time as the police charged him with something. "I think they have a lot to choose from. Did you hear that he's not supposed to leave the building with one of us in charge? I wonder how they didn't know that."

"It sounded to me like he was doing a lot of things that they didn't know about. Hopefully, they fire him. But probably they'll send him to anger management school and be done with it. Worse things have happened." She thought he might be right about the anger management classes. She'd read that someplace how people who worked for the place that she had were sending their 'family members' to classes rather than wasting all the time that they paid for training for them. Yes, she thought, worse things have happened.

"Why are you here?" She still thought that he was somewhat blurry, but didn't say that to him. The nurses had asked if she wanted anything for pain, and when she got it, she realized that the man had been there with her all day. And now it was nearly nine o'clock, and he was still hanging around. "You have to have better things to do than to just sit around a hospital bed all evening."

"What do you know about shifters?" She said that she knows that she works with a couple, but other than that, she didn't know anything. "They mate for life, did you know that much?"

"No. And why would I care? I'm just a plain

human who has been hurt. You didn't answer my question." He said that he was her mate and that he belonged to her. "Belong to me? What does that even mean? And I don't want a mate. I have my things and my life just the way I want them to be."

"I'm afraid that it doesn't work that way. I've found you or you've found me, I'm not sure how you want to say that, and you're stuck with me." She rolled to her side and didn't look at him. "We don't have to talk about this now. I know you must be hurting."

"As I said, I have things the way that I like them, and I'm not going to be bossed around by you. You can take your mate business someplace else. I don't want you." He laughed again, and she was beginning to think there was something wrong with him. "Go away. I've had a really shitty day today, and I don't need you and your laughing ass here with me."

"That's very hurtful. And I have no intentions of bossing you around. I know you have a life. While you were out on the floor, one of your coworkers said you were going to college to become a lawyer. I was one of those at one time. I don't remember how long ago—what's the matter?" She turned in the bed to look at him.

"I just realized who you are. You're one of the Savage guys. The cousins or something along those lines. You're supposed to have more money than Midas, as my grannie says." He didn't bother denying it. "I don't need some rich guy trying to make me into his plaything either. I have a life that I like just fine." He laughed. This time, it was as if he'd gotten a really good kick out of her woes. "You're certifiable. Has anyone ever told you that before?"

"My brother, Brenin, said that I do laugh when things around me aren't that funny. But sometimes I get a kick out of what people are saying, so I laugh." She rolled back to her side, careful of her ribs this time. "I think you're beautiful and will fit right in with my family, Raven."

"We'll see." She had to roll to her back; her ribs were hurting her too badly to sleep on her side. "We're not having sex. I draw the line at being your plaything." When he laughed again, she willed herself to sleep. The man was insane if he thought that she'd just come along nicely with him.

~*~

Standing up, he stretched when he knew she was asleep. Cassian thought that having a mate was fun so far. Of course, she was going to be tough to make her believe that he wasn't going to boss her around. Also, she wasn't going to be a plaything either. He thought that was funny that she was so dead set against having him in her life that he caught himself smiling every once in a while just thinking about her.

Daniel was lucky that there had been people around when he'd realized that Raven was his mate.

He might well have shifted and killed him right where he stood. He'd been eating in the little fast-food place when he noticed that everyone was standing by the door to the parking lot. There wasn't any way that he could have reacted quicker, as he was shocked to see what the man was doing to the woman. The man was beating her and knocking her to the ground like she was nothing more than a stick.

Walking into the hallway where the nurses were, he nodded to one of them when they asked if everything was all right. The only reason he'd been able to stay was because Kings had pulled a few strings for him in order to get himself a free pass to stay in Raven's room. He couldn't leave her, not injured the way that she was.

Every time he looked at her face, his dragon wanted to find the man responsible and kill him. Not just wound him like he'd done to Raven, but to rip his throat out and stomp on him as his dragon. The doctors said she'd be all right, but it didn't lessen the fact that he'd beaten an innocent woman like he had.

Cassian had met men like Daniel before. Given a little bit of power over someone, it went straight to their heads. Daniel was the kind of man that the police were forever screening for with tests to keep them out of their departments. They would abuse their power and people, too. It was worse that they were able to carry a gun.

Walking the floor, he was careful not to make any kind of disruption for the nurses. They were all working hard, and he didn't want to get in their way. Going back to the room that Raven was in, he sat down on one of the nice loungers and set it up so that it was leaning back for him. Closing his eyes, he thought about what Raven was going to bring to his life. He could already feel a bit more magic around his body and was happy for that. The need to heal her was paramount, but he held off. People would be questioning everything if she were suddenly healed up from her beating. His body tensed up when he thought of the damage that had been done to her.

She had two broken ribs and several that were badly bruised. Her wrist was broken, and she had several cuts on her face that had needed stitches. There was a long jagged cut on her head where she hit the car, they told him, and that had required seventeen stitches on its own. It was also the point where she'd been concussed as well. Her legs and other arm were cut up, and she had both her eyes blackened, and her nose was bruised. She was, in a word, a mess. And all because some jackass had decided that he had power over her and was going to make her do what he wanted.

Every time he thought of Daniel, he wanted to kill him. Which wasn't helping him sleep. He had a big day tomorrow, and being worked up wasn't going to make it easier on him. Tomorrow, he was going to have to work hard in convincing his new mate that he'd never do her any harm and that she'd be safe with him. He would even make sure that her grannie was all right.

The elderly woman couldn't make it to the hospital until tomorrow. Her driver for the day, a next-door neighbor who took her to appointments and such, was in for the night and didn't drive after dark. He was going to send someone for her first thing in the morning and make sure that she could see her granddaughter before she was released. She'd been ever so grateful that he'd called her.

It was Kaida who had gotten the idea that someone needed to call for her. She'd rummaged through her mind gently and had found that she'd been living with her grannie. Getting the phone number was easy after that. Someone at the police station had known about her grannie and had given him the number to call her. Cassian remembered the conversation well.

"You tell me what time you get up in the morning, and I'll have a car there waiting to bring you in. Then, when you've had enough visiting, I'll get one to send you home in, too. No point in bothering your neighbor when I can easily do this for you." She told him she was up at six in the morning. "How about I have the car there at seven, that way you can have plenty of time to get going and have some breakfast too."

"That sounds about good to me." He told her his name twice, but he wasn't worried about her not remembering it. She was stressed, and he knew it. "She's all I've got in the whole world. Well, I suppose that's not true. I do have my daughter, but she ain't worth nothing. I don't think she's even seen her daughter since I won custody of her all those years ago. Her daddy neither." She snorted as she spoke to him about Raven. "Sorrier bunch of people you'd ever want to know. Not that you'd want them around. They forever had their hands out all the time until they had to start paying me some money to keep my girl. Not that I would have ever charged them, but the courts said they had to, so I got me a check from the two of them every month like clockwork."

She had a terrible laugh. It was like a braying jackass that had been startled from behind. But he'd bet anything that she didn't care. She made no apologies about it and seemed to enjoy laughing about things. It made him smile when she laughed the first time.

"I'll take good care of the two of you, too. You don't have to worry about anything so long as I'm around." And he'd be around forever, too, he wanted to tell her, but didn't. He didn't know her all that well as yet. "She's not going to be able to be alone after she leaves the hospital, so I'll have the two of you stay with me until she's better. All right?"

She said it was fine, but he could hear the confusion in her voice. He'd be that way, too, if some stranger told you that he was going to take you home with your hurt granddaughter. Getting up when Raven stirred around on the bed, he made sure that she wasn't in any pain so that she could rest. Giving her just enough magic that would keep her in a deeper sleep so that she could heal faster.

At midnight, they came in to wake her and ask her some questions. It was protocol for head injuries, and he understood that. He didn't have to like it, but he did understand why they did it. To make sure that the injury wasn't getting any worse.

Just as he was settling back down in the chair, Bluebonnet came to see him. He had been wondering how they were getting along at his home, and she assured him that things were coming along nicely. She was also able to give him his laptop as well as the two books he'd been reading that were by his bedside. Blue smiled at him when he thanked her.

"I will have fresh clothing for you in the morning, should you wish it." He said that he would and thanked her again. "Would you like for me to bring you any food? There is plenty at the house that I can make sure you have. It will be no problem should you wish for something from a restaurant either."

"I'm fine right now. I'll get something here for breakfast before Mrs. Lanning shows up. She's

Raven's grandmother on her mother's side." Blue told him that she'd been in Raven's mind and she's been able to make the master bedroom to her liking. "That's something that I wouldn't have thought of. If there is anything you need, just let me know, and I can get it for you. She should be fine once she's able to get out of here."

"That's wonderful news, my lord." She asked him about things at the house, and he was able to tell her what was going on. He also told her about the room that she was using for herself and the other faeries. It was a big room, and he didn't mind them setting up a small place for them to have crafts, too. They all made their own furniture. "They are loving the room and the setup. Some of them have been starting on larger homes because of how much room they have. I'm so happy for them."

"I'll need to get a faerie for Raven so that she can have the same benefits that I do. The magic cannot heal her as yet. There are police involved in her getting hurt, and they might not understand if she was suddenly well. But I would like for her to have a connection with someone so that if something ever happens, we can get to her much faster than I was able to today." She asked what had happened, and he told her. "So you can see that she's going to need time to heal on her own and not raise any questions about her injuries. Understand?"

"I do my lord. We don't want her to be

questioned about the manner in which she was able to heal. Humans don't understand that at all." There was a great deal that humans didn't understand, but since his mate was one of them, he was fine with that. The less they knew, the better off every shifter would be. Especially those with a closed mind. He'd seen plenty of those in his lifetime, too. People who only saw things that they thought were real. "I shall return to the house now, sire, if there is no more need of me this evening."

After sending her on her way, he sat back and looked at things on his computer. He wasn't really concentrating on anything, so when he saw the article about Raven getting hurt, he was watching the video that accompanied it twice before he realized that it was her.

It was small wonder he didn't do more damage to her human body the way that he was treating her. All that did was get his anger up again, and it took another walk around the floor to get himself to calm down. He was hoping that Daniel would get out of jail. He was going to teach him a few lessons in how to treat a woman. Especially his woman.

Chapter 1

Daniel didn't know why he had to be in these stupid classes when he'd done nothing wrong. Of course, he had hit Raven a great deal, but all she had to do was stay over for him to go to the bank and some other errands that he had to do, and none of this would have happened. Because of her, he'd had to spend six weeks in these classes—like he needed anger management classes, he thought that he handled his need to be pissed off just fine. This was all her fault.

"Mr. Daniel, are you paying attention to Mr. Carl?" He said that he was thinking about what he'd say if it were his turn. Which wasn't a lie, he wanted to tell them all to get a life. "You'll have your turn tomorrow, like I told you earlier. Pay attention to Mr. Carl and see what progress he's made with his classes."

"Yes, ma'am." He didn't like being called by his first name either. He was Mr. Winters at work, and he saw no reason why he wasn't called that in these unreasonable classes. He had better things to do with his time than to sit around and listen to people talk about how they shouldn't have been so angry about whatever brought them to these classes. He knew who had brought him to these classes, and he was going to make sure she understood that he was in charge as soon as he got back to work.

He couldn't believe that he was going to keep his job after this. He'd beaten a woman nearly to death, and they said that he was under stress at work and needed a second chance. What he needed was better workers, like Raven had been, and things would run themselves. But he was stuck with a bunch of kids who couldn't get off their asses to make a living. As soon as he passed his final test, he'd be free to go back to his job and order around all the subordinates that worked for him.

He'd not worked out how to get to Raven. Her last day had been the day of the great beating — what he called the day he'd been arrested. That was another thing that pissed him off. She wasn't willing for him to talk her into staying at work indefinitely, and he would get the fat bonus of a thousand dollars to not quit and work for him. What did she want to go to college for in the first place? Being an attorney wasn't anything that she'd be good at. She was just a stupid worker who made minimum wage. Perhaps a bit more than that, as she was the lead cashier. Stupid woman.

Daniel didn't like that she was a few months older than he was, either. Not that she ever rubbed it into his face or anything like that. But she was older, and that pissed him off to no end. Everyone else who worked for him was nothing but teenagers, and he liked lording over them when he wanted to. She knew all the rules, too, that he was supposed to have been following. He hated her with a passion.

"Mr. Daniel?" He looked around the room before looking at the woman in charge of the classes. "Did you want to stay over and speak to me about something? I've heard you grumbling a bit. Are you still mad at the young woman who you say made it so that you had to do these classes? She had nothing to do with you having to take these classes. You brought this all on yourself."

"I was just wondering how I would get in touch with her to make amends." He felt laughter bubble up from his gut and nearly spilled it out with the thought of making restitution to anyone. "You did say that I was supposed to tell the people that I hurt that I was sorry."

"Yes, but you have to mean it. And I believe that Ms. Raven has moved on from her job working for the restaurant. She's making a life of her own now that she can get around better on her own." He wanted to ask her what had happened to Raven, what sort of wounds he had given her, but no one would answer that. They said that he was in a stress-induced rage and that was all he needed to know. Damned stupid people. "You just concentrate on getting yourself better, and we'll work out something else for you to make amends with her."

"I just want to make sure she knows how sorry I am." Sorry that he didn't beat her more. But then there had been that big fella that had knocked him off of her and out. He didn't remember any other time in his life when someone had been able to get the better of him in a fist fight. "Can't you find her someplace from where she's going to college or something? I feel it's my duty to tell her that I'm sorry."

"We'll cross that bridge when we come to it. Right now you need to pay more attention in classes and share more. I know you said you had a headache at those first two meetings, but it's been three now, and you should be better. Just remember that's the consequence of something that you did when you chose to hit that young lady." He said that he remembered and gently touched his face. Both his eyes were still black from the punch to his face, and his nose was never going to be the same. Another person that he wanted to make amends to was the guy who punched him for no reason. "See? You're drifting off right now. You're going to have to pay more attention to the people around you, or you'll never pass these classes."

"I'm paying attention." Frustrated and trying his best not to show it, Daniel went about his business of packing up his things to take back to the jail cell with him. The officer in charge of him wouldn't help him carry all the things that he had to carry, and he thought that was just ridiculous of him. They made him carry his jacket because heaven forbid he had to wear his suit to classes when everyone else was wearing their jogging pants and shorts to these meetings. But he was in upper management and had to look the part. More stupid people, who he just didn't understand.

On his way back to the jail cell, he thought of the day of the great beating. It hadn't been anything that he'd started out wanting to do. Just hit her a couple of times to make sure that she knew that he was in charge. He found that he liked making her bleed. It wasn't the pain that he got such a rush from, but seeing the blood flowing from whatever wounds he put to her, mostly on her face. He also hoped that she'd be scarred too from what he'd done to her. She'd had such a pretty face.

His cell had been cleaned while he'd been out. Which meant that they mopped his floor and took the sheets off his bed. There were clean ones that he had to put back on, but he wasn't in the mood for that right now. He had to figure out how to get to Raven.

Raven had been a model employee when she was working. Never late, always kept the dining room cleaned up. And she wasn't afraid of a little hard work either. She'd been working at the place longer than anyone and had been asked to take over the management job, but declined. She didn't want to have to be bothered with it. Well, he loved being in charge and the thrill it gave him to lord over the people who were beneath him. And the sooner she learned that he was far superior to her, the better things would be for her. If she ever came back to work for him, that was.

He didn't like that she'd gotten away from him. He wanted her to be his subject, and she had made him angry. Sitting on his cot, he thought about the day of the great beating and wondered why he'd been so angry with her. She'd been off when he told her that she was going to stay after, and he shouldn't have tried to get her to stay. Christ, when he thought of how angry he'd been, it made him slightly sick. Not that he'd not do it all over again if given the chance.

"Dinner." He watched as his tray was sent into his room by sliding it across the floor. He'd just wait until the officer was gone before he'd bend down and pick it up. It was little mind games he played with himself that got him through the day. "You have to make your bed. Get it done before lights out, or you'll be doing it in the dark again."

He said he'd get it done and decided to do it before he ate. There was no point in pissing off the police today; he had better things to do other than put up with their rules, too. Once he had the bed made as well as he knew how, he pulled his meal to him and opened the lids. He had to admit that the food here was good. Tonight he was having a hamburger with French fries and a large wedge of pie for dessert. He didn't eat like this at his own home, much less at work, where he got a free meal every time he worked.

After eating, he laid down on his cot and thought about what he was going to do when he got out of here. He was going to have to suck up a little more, or he'd be taking the classes until he was an old man. He didn't see himself as a fast food manager for long. He wanted to run his own district so that he could have more minions beneath him. Smiling to himself, he wondered if he could get the same district as the one he was working in now. It would be a feather in his cap to have come up from the ranks and been the best district manager that there ever was.

That wasn't something that he thought about too often. He had this anger management thing hanging over his head, and he wanted to make good on his promise to give it his best shot at getting out of the classes. He had plenty of things that he could work around, and one of them was to suck up to everyone that he could. There was no point in trying to be a good manager. He just wanted to be able to rule over the people who were beneath him.

~*~

Cassian didn't know what to do with his free time. He'd been making sure that Raven was all right in getting around for the past three weeks, and she was doing so much better than before. Now he wanted to keep an eye on her, but she kept pushing him away. It was sort of hurtful to him how she didn't seem to want him around. But he was in love with her, and he was going to try his best to make this work out.

She'd been beaten so badly about a month ago by her former boss. Raven had given her notice to the company, but her former boss wanted her to stay over, and she'd had plans. He didn't know what her plans had been, but it didn't matter; there was no reason for him to beat her up like he had. If not for his intervention, there is no telling how much worse it would have been for her.

"There's a man at the door for you." He watched as she limped her way out of his office and into the hall as she continued. "I don't know who he is, but he said that it was important that he speak to you."

"I'll come to him." He stood up and made his way around his desk to go to the front door when Raven turned and looked at him. "Is there something wrong? You know that I'd give you the world if I could."

"Daniel Winters is going to anger management classes, and they let him keep his job. Why would anyone think that people would want to work for him after what he did to me?" He said that he'd been keeping an eye on him with a faerie and knew that he wasn't doing so well in the classes. "I don't doubt that. He's a monster."

When she went on her way towards the kitchen, he watched her. She really was getting around much better than before, and he was happy for her. Going to the front door, he opened it to find Ace standing on the steps with a huge smile on his face.

"You should have told her to let you in. Come on in and tell me how your job is going. Do you need my help on anything?" Ace Savage was his cousin from the same side of the family. He'd run for mayor a few months ago and had been voted in. The previous mayor, Morgan Trail, of all names, had been doing nothing in office, and Ace was getting so much done already. Even the sidewalks looked much better than they had before he'd taken office. "I was just in my office doing some trading on the stock market. Come in and tell me what you've been up to."

"I came to ask you if there was maybe a way that you could help me find more money for the city. The football field is in good repair, but the housing that they use for the sale of food and drinks is in poor shape. I don't know that it'll go for another season." They ended up at the desk in his office with Ace sitting across from him. "I don't know what that would even be called, funding for the football vending."

"We'll try that first." He put that in and had a few hits on it. "It says here that we can get funding for the building, but we'd have to show proof that it's all it's used for. I don't think there will be a problem with that. I know they use it all seasons to keep the families that come there fed."

"They want to expand, too. I'm not sure how much room there is to do that, but it would be nice if they didn't have to put pans around when it rains. I guess it's quite a flood even when it's just a little bit of rain." He brought up the specs on the grant and told Ace what he had to do. "Tank is the one who is going to be applying for the grant. He's having so much fun finding money that I think that he's having more fun than I am. And I can't believe how much money is out there for small towns to use. A lot of things could have been finished and fixed had Morgan just looked on the internet for stuff to pay for it."

He had a feeling that Ace was there for another reason and decided to wait him out. While the website was printing off the computer, he made small talk about how Raven was getting along. Ace seemed to be about half listening to him when he suddenly looked at him, concerned.

"Something has come to my attention. It's not terrible, but it's enough that I'm worried about the effects it'll have on the area. Did you know that someone is buying up land around here?" He said that it was Tucker. Tucker had been buying up land for the last several years. "Do you think that he is going to do something with it that will cause trouble for the taxpayers?"

"He's hoping that if he gets enough land purchased, he'll be able to bring more businesses to town. I don't know if you're aware of this or not, but the big manufacturing business out on Route Sixty has finally filled up. He's hoping that soon, he'll have enough to get something else around in here. I heard, too, that the schools are coming along nicely. That's his baby, too."

"Kings said that I should ask Tucker, but he frightens me a bit. He's such a big man, and he rarely smiles. I don't think he likes me all that much." He told Ace that he's bored with his life outside of being with his little dragon, Kaida. "I heard that he called her that all the time. They're a good couple."

"They are. And I think he'd be hurt if he knew what you thought about him. He's really a good guy and I love him." He said that he'd go and talk to him when he was finished here. "You really should. He's about the nicest person that I know, and other than my brother, someone that I depend on a great deal."

"Good to know. I'll work on getting to know him better." Ace stood up. "I have a couple of meetings in the morning through lunch tomorrow. Why don't you come by the office and help me figure out the mess that the other mayor left behind for me? He's not one for filing something, is what I've come to realize."

"I'd love to come out and help you." The two of them hugged, and Ace left him to go back to his office. He had no doubt that they'd be breaking ground on a new shelter for the vending at the fields in no time. Ace was the perfect man for the job of mayor, and he loved that he'd been a part of him getting into office. He went to find Raven to tell her of his plans.

"Did you want to go and get dinner tonight with your grannie? I heard that she really likes pizza subs, and I know just the place to get them where they're really good." She said that she was trying to get around without the support of the cane. "I'll be there for you. I can carry you, too, if you'd rather not walk all that far."

"I don't need you to carry me. I walk just fine by myself. I just tire quickly. I think that it's because I've been down for so long." She looked up at him. "Why are you so nice to me all the time? I'm trying my best to push you away, yet you do something like offering to carry me places, and I can't stand that. You're making it difficult for me to hold you at arm's length."

"I'm hoping that you no longer want to hold me away from you. That I might wear you down a bit more daily." He wanted to kiss her, but had a feeling that she'd knock him out. She tended to be slightly violent when she was backed into a corner. "I've fallen in love with you, Raven, and would do anything in the world to make you happy with me and create an us."

"I don't know what to do if we were to become an us." He told her that he understood that very well. It was a lot for her to take in. "See? You're being nice to me again when I would have kicked my ass if I said anything like that to me." He wasn't quite sure if that was what she meant to say, but left it alone.

"Would you like to have dinner with me and your grannie? Right now, that's all I'll ask of you." She turned away, but not before turning back, telling him that she'd love to have dinner with him and her grannie. "I think your grannie likes me. She sure is a wonderful person to have around, isn't she?"

"I've always thought so. She took me in when my parents divorced. I had a choice to live with either one that I wanted, and I chose her. My parents were pissed off at me, so they didn't visit when they had the time to do so. They were also mad that they had to pay her child support over the years, too." He asked if she had anything to do with them now that she was older. "No. I haven't seen either of them since I was ten. They'd messed up weekends on coming to get me. It was a court order that they visit me, and when they both showed up, it was a fight. After that, they just stopped coming around. I was fine by then. I figured out that I needed them less and less over the years than I needed my grannie. She's been my lifeline all this time."

"Another reason to love her." He asked if she wanted to eat in the house or go out, and she said that if he drove her to the pizza place, she could walk in. "All right. I'll make sure that everything is ready to go at about six. If you get too tired, please don't hesitate to ask for help. I'm there for you."

"I know you are." She made her way down the hall again, and he was surprised to see a faerie following her. He knew that one of them was going to be her forever faerie, but he'd not heard that she'd found one. Choosing a faerie was a big deal to the little creatures, and they didn't take their job lightly.

Kings and Skye had been chosen to be the king and queen of their kind. He'd not wanted the job any more than Skye did, and they went to the Lady Earth to tell her that they didn't want the job. As one of the perks that they would get is a couple of pips—a group of faeries—to help around the house. When it got to be too many for them, they decided that all of them should have faeries in their homes to help out, too. It had been overwhelming at first, having so many of them needing to be put to work, but they soon found a job for one another, and he loved having them around to keep up with the daily chores around the house. The Lady Earth had decided that they could keep the faeries around so that they could help them when they needed. He loved that it had worked out so well.

He had his own faerie, too; her name was Cup Cake, and they got along very well. He supposed that he should have seen to Raven having one, but it hadn't occurred to him, and he felt bad about it. He did wonder if Grannie would need one as well and decided to ask one of them when he saw one of them again.

The rest of the afternoon, he fielded questions

for his cousins and his brother, Brenin. They were a close lot and worked well together. One of the things that he was asked by his cousin Tucker was when the pool was going to be dug up and redone. He knew the answer to that because he'd asked Ace when he'd been over this morning.

"They're going to start the deconstruction tomorrow, as a matter of fact. They'd had it drained and were waiting for approval from the city to get started. Ace approved their work just yesterday." He asked if they were going to be able to make the pool larger than it was. "Yes, there is enough money in the budget to get the pool enlarged to about twice its size, as well as have the handicapped lift that started the whole thing put in as well. There will be enough money left over that we'll be able to put in two lifeguard stations as well as a full bathroom for showering and changing."

"That's wonderful news. I'm so glad that one of us was able to find the funding that was needed to have the entire thing redone." He said that Ace is the one who got the ball rolling. "And will it be done by spring? I heard that they're going to be selling memberships to people for the chance to use the pool as a party place during the summer months."

"The memberships won't be that much. And it's only there to help defray the costs of hiring lifeguards to be at the pool year-round." He thought that was a brilliant idea. "That's on Tank. He also has a flyer going out that says that the city will pay for anyone who wants to be a lifeguard, so long as they work one summer for us. I think that will get a lot of kids applying for the job."

"I noticed that the sidewalks are being redone, too. I hate that they had to cut down all the trees along the main street, but planting them had been what messed the sidewalks up in the first place. Also, I have to tell you, it was nice not seeing the Christmas décor hanging from the light poles along Main Street, too." Cassian said it had been the first thing that Ace had done when he became mayor. "He's right on top of things. I have to set up a meeting with him about some businesses that might like to come to town." He told him about the conversation that he'd had with Ace just this morning. "I didn't know that he felt that way towards me."

"I think he'd be embarrassed if you were to bring it up to him. Just go and talk to him about your plans for the businesses, and things will smooth out. You have been under a lot of stress of late. I was wondering about that too." He told him what was going on. "I'm sorry you didn't say anything sooner, Tucker. I would have taken on some extra projects so that you could spend some time with Kaida."

"I hate to bother you because you just found your mate, too. I didn't want to ask you to take away time from her." He said they were still at the getting-to-know-one-another stage and still were feeling each other out. "Good. Take your time with that. You won't regret that at all."

Cassian found Cup Cake in his office when he came back from lunch. He asked about Grannie having a faerie too, and he said that he'd get onto that. He said that Bo was the faerie for Raven and that they were getting along nicely. He was happy for that. And then wondered about any magic that she'd gotten.

"She discovered that she could change her clothing at will. That was a big hit, she told me. Not having to sort through her closet when she needs to change is wonderful." He smiled and said that he liked that perk too. "Also, she hadn't noticed until it was pointed out to her, but she can bring things to her as well. The first time it happened, it startled both her and Bo. But she's getting used to the other things that are popping up for her."

"Good. I wanted to have a talk with her about dragons, but she's been falling asleep so quickly after dinner that I've put it off for her to rest instead." Cup Cake thought that was a wonderful idea. "But she does seem to be getting stronger daily, and the wounds on her face are nearly gone."

"We despaired of her never wanting to leave the house again when she saw her face in the hospital. She was quite beaten up from that man." He told her about the anger management classes that he was taking. "Yes,

we've been to a few of them. He's been warned that
he's not going to pass the tests if he doesn't pay more
attention. His mind is on the young miss still, and how
she'd gotten away with getting him in the classes in the
first place. He blames her for his lot in life."

"I didn't know that you had anyone on him.
Thank you for that." He told him that Lord Kings
had set it up and was glad to have done it. "Keep me
informed as to what else he's up to when he's taking
the classes. I don't want him to be able to harm my
mate again."

"He'll never get past any of us, my lord."
Nodding once, he was glad that someone was taking
care that Daniel was being watched and felt bad that
he'd not been the one who set it up. He was going to
have to be more on the ball from now on if he wanted to
keep his mate and her grannie safe. "If there is nothing
else, I'll take care to get the things finished up on your
list for you. It's my pleasure to have been able to ease
your mind about your lovely mate. She's a joy to be
around."

"I agree. Just keep me updated on Daniel." She
said that she would and flittered away. He'd have to
thank Kings for keeping up with the goings on with
Daniel and make sure that he got updates from him. If
he was still thinking about Raven, then he was going
to have to do his best to not allow him near her again.
In two weeks, she was going to begin her online classes

from here to start on her journey to becoming the best attorney there was. He was so proud of her that he could have burst each time she kept him updated on things that she had going on as well.

Dinner was a good time. Raven did allow him to help her back to the car, but only because it had started to rain and the sidewalks were slick. She didn't want to undo all the work that she'd done to get her to the point where she was, and he didn't blame her. The sooner she was in good health, the better for everyone, he thought.

That night, when she made her way up to bed, he stayed downstairs and locked up the house. He wasn't worried about anyone breaking in, but he did worry about people thinking that he was an easy target. He'd never locked his doors before. His thinking was that if they did break in, he'd just shift to his dragon and kill them. Then no one would break into his house again, he figured.

As he made his way to his bedroom, he thought that he'd get with his cousins and fly tomorrow night. It was the only time that they could do it, and they could see better in the darkness than they could during the daylight hours as their great beasts. He was excited about getting together with them and decided that they needed to do it more often. It was really great to be his other self and know that the others felt the same way.

Chapter 2

Raven didn't much care for the doctor she was seeing. He creeped her out a bit, and he touched her too much. When she'd said as much to Skye when she'd come with her today, she said that she should nip it in the bud before he got out of hand. Or Cassian would kill him.

"He really wouldn't kill him, would he?" Skye told her that they were a very jealous group of beings, and they protected what they thought of as theirs. "But to kill him because I think he's getting to be a little too familiar with me is a bit insane."

"Had Cassian known that you were his mate when he knocked Daniel out, he would have killed him right then and there. I think that the man is lucky that he didn't know. We'd still be talking about the great dragon that killed a man for knocking you around." They both laughed, but Raven wasn't sure whether she was kidding or not. It was nice to be protected, but to kill a man who was getting a little too fresh with her? She didn't see it. "Have you seen his dragon yet? They're going to go flying tonight, and you'll get the chance to see him then. All of them, as a matter of fact.

Kings' dragon is the biggest because he was supposed to be the king of our kind, but since he's turned that down, he got to keep the power and magic that went with it."

"Cassian told me about that. They just gave him the power to be king and did not even ask them if they wanted to do it. I think I would have turned it down, too. It sounds like a great deal of work all the time." Skye said they wouldn't have had any quality of life outside of doing the work for the kingdom. "I can see that too. I like having you and the others around. It's nice to be able to talk to you when I have a question."

"Lady Earth has been answering a lot of questions for me, too. She created dragons so that the magic that she has would be spread out all over the world. Kings and I both agreed that if they'd gone this long without a king and queen, they could surely go a few more decades without one until the right person came along."

They talked about the Connors then, too. She'd heard about them and how they had killed Trevor's parents — Trevor was the boy who lived with Kings and Skye until they could adopt him. How they'd wanted to kill Skye, too, by hiring out Jason Waggoner to get the boy from her and kill her at the same time. Their trial was coming up soon, and she had heard enough about them that she wanted them out of the way as well. They were dangerous to have around.

"Jason confessed to killing fifty plus women and men when he'd been in jail. He tried to take his confession back, but since he'd told them where he'd buried all the bodies, no one would believe him. He'll more than likely get several life sentences." She asked about the Conners. "They killed Trevor's parents when he was about one so that they could have his magic to get money from the stock market. When he'd run away, he met up with me on the run, too, from Jason, and he decided that he was going to kill me, too, for the reward of getting Trevor back to the Connors. It didn't work out that well for any of them."

"No, I guess not." The two of them were getting along nicely when Kaida joined them. She was so nice and sweet that it was difficult for her to remember that she had all this power at her disposal. She was sure that Skye did as well, but she never used it around her, so she didn't know how much she had. Upon thinking about that, she remembered that she was supposed to be the queen of dragons and her magic would be a great bit too. She asked Skye about the baby she was going to have soon.

"It's a dragon. A friend of Kings came to talk to me about having a dragon baby. It's not all that hard to do, I'm beginning to see. Once I have the egg, it will grow with the baby for about a year, and then we'll have a baby dragon that can shift from birth. No matter who the guys mate with, whether it's a shifter or not, the babies will always be dragons. Isn't that cool?"

They talked about the baby for a while. Skye was practically glowing from the knowledge of having a baby with Kings. And the faeries were excited to have a newborn around, too. There was a great deal of magic surrounding a newborn that they were all vying for the opportunity to help raise it. She just wanted to see the baby when it was born in the event that someday she and Cassian decided to have one. If they ever got to that point.

She didn't talk too much about Cassian's and her relationship. They didn't have one as yet, and she felt embarrassed that she kept him from touching her. He couldn't even get close to her enough so that they were breathing the same air. It wasn't that she was afraid of him, just the opposite, as a matter of fact. But she was still biding her time in getting close to him in the event that he turned into someone who wanted to boss her around. So far, he'd not done that, but she was ever watchful.

After the three of them were finished with their meals, they talked about the upcoming things that were going on around the little town. It was the place she was getting her information about Cassian, too. And what he did with the family to keep them in money and jobs around town. Cassian had been an attorney long ago and knew a bit about contracts, so he was the go-to person who would read them over when there were questions. She wanted to be able to help them out like that for all the times they'd been there for her so far.

Yesterday, she'd been in town mailing some letters and stuff for college. Brenin had been going there too and gave her a ride back to the house when she was finished. Everyone had been so nice to her that she was having a hard time keeping them from hurting her when they decided that she wasn't really Cassian's mate and nothing more than an injured girl that just happened to have some kind of scent that called to him. Whatever the reason was, she was slightly nervous about getting too close to any of them for fear that she would be friendless if they ever figured out that she wasn't his mate.

"You have magic, don't you?" She said that she did. "That's a sure sign that you're his mate. And the longer you're around him, the more you'll get. You'll get some if you haven't already gotten some from the other men, too, as you go along."

"I'm not sure I can figure out what to do with more magic. The little bit that I've been playing around with has been great for me." She asked about healing. "I haven't healed yet, and I thought that was one of the perks of having a magical mate."

"He's more than likely holding off on healing you so that the police don't get into why you healed so quickly. It'll be good for your court date, too, when you have to face Winters as well." She said she'd not thought of that. "I didn't either when I was with Kings at first. He could have healed me from my bruising, too, but held off. I think that it hurt him more than it did me to not help. They're all like that. They seemed to know when you're hurting, too. Mentally or physically."

"It's all a lot, isn't it? I mean, I was just working in a fast food place, and now look at me. I have magic and a mate that I know nothing about." She told her to ask him what she wanted to know. "He seems so busy all the time. I don't want to disturb him any."

"He's more than likely busy so that he doesn't annoy you all the time." Both women laughed, and she didn't understand what was going on. "He wants you in the most cardinal way and is avoiding you by working so you don't think he's pressuring you into anything. They're really good about that as well."

After lunch and on her way home, she thought about what they'd told her. It was like the magic was a lot to deal with. She'd never been so confused in her life, and she thought that she had a good head on her shoulders. As she was letting herself into the house, she thought of Bo, and when she opened the door, there he was. Smiling at the little man, she asked him what he'd been up to today.

"Nothing much, my lady. I've been going over the paperwork for your college classes. If you don't mind me saying so, I'm very proud to be your servant.

You're very brilliant for wanting to go to college to educate yourself." She felt her face heat up and thanked him. "I have marked places on some of the forms where you'll need to sign off on them. Also, the money that is in the account, lord Cassian told me to explain to you that it was yours to use."

"Where is lord Cassian today?" He told her that he was in the office working on contracts that he'd been given by Lord Tucker. "He's been doing that a great deal. Is there a reason that he's working so hard?"

The little man blushed from the tip of his toes to the top of his head. And his wings, usually fluttering like those of a butterfly, were going so quickly that it was difficult for her to see them. She shouldn't have embarrassed him, but it was easier for her to talk to him than it was to her own mate. Making a decision, she entered the office after knocking.

Cassian had his head down and looked like he was concentrating hard on whatever he was doing. Clearing her throat had him looking up, but he didn't say anything. She wondered if this was a good idea.

"I wanted to talk to you." He smiled at her, and all her anxiousness seemed to melt away. "It's about us. I was wondering how sure you were that I'm your mate. And what sort of things do you have planned for me now that we're living together?"

"I don't understand the question. What do you mean by plans for you?" She told him what she thought. "I'm not going to make you do anything. You've got a good head on your shoulders and don't seem to need me to watch over you all the time. As for us living together, I thought that you and your grannie liked living here."

"I do. We do." She asked if she could sit down. When he told her that she could, she went to the chair that was just across from his desk and flopped into it. She was letting her frustrations be known, and he seemed to not understand them. "I know nothing about you. You've always got your head into something from your cousins and brother. Not that I'm mad about that, but I don't know when I can bother you."

"Anytime you wish. I'm here for you." To make a point, she supposed he stacked up all the paperwork on his desk and leaned back in his chair. "Anytime I'm here, I'm open for you to talk to me. What is it you'd like to know?"

"How did you become a dragon and why?" He told her that he was born a dragon because his parents had decided to have a hatchling. He also told her that he didn't think they really wanted him; it was just something that happened to them. "You had a sister."

"We did. Her name was Margo, and she was meaner than a rattlesnake. Just as sneaky, too. Some time ago, she and Skye got into a pissing match, and she drew first blood. With an enemy, as in a dragon enemy, whoever draws first blood owns not just their human form, but their dragon must do what they wish as well. All Skye did was turn her over to us, Brenin and me, and we got to treat her how we wanted. However, that didn't last long; we're nothing like she was, and we allowed her to be taken care of by the counsel. She'd been killing other dragons and humans for gain for a long time, and it caught up with her." Raven asked him if he missed her. "Not really. I think about her once in a while, but I don't miss her. She wasn't a good person to be around. I'm glad that she's gone so that I don't have to keep looking over my shoulder all the time to see where she is."

"Are you older than your brother?" He said that they were ten days apart and that he'd been born first. "Do dragons usually have two or more babies? The reason I ask is because Skye is getting large with her child, and I wondered if it could be twins."

"She's just having the one egg. I might not have known that before, but Kings had a friend of his come to the house to talk to her about having a baby dragon. She'll carry the egg for six months or so, then the hatchling will take a year to grow big enough to be hatched. The egg is small when it's first born, but it will grow with the egg so that she's not having a large egg that might harm her." He asked if she was hungry. "I'm starved. Sometimes I forget to eat lunch when I'm working. How about we head to the kitchen and you tell me about yourself, too."

"There isn't much to tell. My parents divorced when I was six. They both wanted to have me live with them so that the other would have to pay child support. I'd been staying with my grannie at the time and asked the judge if I could just go on living with her. She loved me. He allowed it, and I've been with her ever since then." She followed him into the kitchen and they had the cook make them both up a tray of meats and cheeses. It was her favorite lunch, and she liked how light it was when she was finished. "I haven't seen them in years. At least a decade or more. I find that I don't care all that much, as they really weren't around for me when I was younger. Grannie and I have a great life together, and we get along well. How old are you?"

"Thousands and thousands of years old. My parents were some of the first family of dragons and the ones who made all the rules. But they became mean with their power, and they were taken care of by the council around the same time that Margo had been. I don't miss them either and am glad, as I said about Margo, I don't have to keep looking over my shoulder all the time. They thought that since I was one of their sons, we had to do what they wanted us to do all the time, and it got old. How do you like this house?"

"I love this house. It's got some fantastic features that I love. The porch is one of my favorite places to hang out when I have some time on my hands. Do you have a lot of money?" He told her that they had a lot of money, as she was his mate, it all belonged to her as well. "What's a lot of money? If I say...say I wanted to not work while going to school, would that be a hardship on us? I'd really like to be able to do that, as that's what I've been saving for all this time."

"You nor I would ever have to work again, and we'd be all right for the next several thousand more years. Which we can live that long, should you wish. You're immortal now, and so is your grannie. I didn't think you wanted to go on in your life without her, so I gave her the magic to be able to take it away should she want." She thanked him for that.

During and after lunch, well into time to have dinner, the two of them talked about whatever popped into their heads. He was able to make it so she wasn't quite so frustrated by answering her questions, and she felt better as time went on. She found herself laughing a good deal more than she'd been doing before and was glad for that as well. She thought that they could become good friends now that they were learning about one another.

~*~

This was his last class, and she was supposed to show up today so that he could tell her how sorry he was. He wasn't, but he'd been making good on his classes so that he could get out of them and onto more important things. Daniel was supposed to start working on Monday, following the last meeting, and he was looking forward to being back there. He knew that things had changed since he'd been gone and knew that he'd have his work cut out for him when he went back to get things back to the way he wanted them to be. Damn it all to fuck and back, why did everyone think that their way was better than what he had in place already?

It wouldn't take him long to get them back in the same way that he'd had them before. All of them thinking that he was their lord and master, and what he said went. Now he had to figure out how to make sure that Raven, the bitch worked for him again so that he could teach her a lesson or two about him being boss.

Getting out of jail today was going to be a biggy. He had hopes of his employees having a nice welcome back party, but so far, no one had mentioned it. He'd been allowed to go to the store once in the last couple of weeks, and he noticed that there were a few new faces whom he could trample on their feelings. No one should be as happy as they seemed to be and work for him. He was going to take that happiness right out of their faces and bring them down to the level that he thought they should be. Right around the floor level.

"Are you ready for this?" He said that he was and was glad that they had brought a cake in for their last meeting. It was for all of them who were going to pass, but he was going to make it all about him, as he usually did. Because, quite frankly, it was all about him all the time. "I've spoken to her as you asked, and she's coming. Not at all thrilled about it, but she'll be there with her husband. I didn't know she'd gotten married until then."

"I heard that she'd met someone but not that she'd married." All the better for her. Her husband would make her listen to him because he'd know the value of having a good-paying job. If they were both working, that was great too. They'd need the money; instead of her not working, she could come back to the restaurant and work for him again. Wouldn't that be the best thing ever? "Are they living in her little apartment? I bet that's sort of cramped up."

"They have a house. Cassian purchased it before he met her, so it's nice for the two of them." A mortgage is even better for him. "Come on, and you can help me set up the meeting for tonight."

He didn't want to help out, but it was better that he did. He wanted to make sure that she was sitting close to him so that he could tell her the way things were going to go from now on. She'd be so twisted up with her new husband that they'd have her working for him again in no time at all.

After the chairs were set up, he looked around for the coffee. He'd become addicted to the stuff since he'd been in jail and the meetings. It was all that kept him awake during them. It wasn't the greatest coffee that he'd ever drank, but it filled the need when he needed something to keep him awake, also to pretend to pay attention.

Daniel thought that he'd done well with the classes despite not wanting or understanding why he was taking them. Of course, he'd gotten a little upset at Raven for not doing what he wanted, and she had been off the clock, but that didn't negate the fact that he'd given her plenty of opportunity to do what he wanted her to do before he'd knocked her around. He'd also enjoyed himself a little too much when she was down and bleeding. Hopefully, he'd be able to make her do both again. He so loved a challenge.

At a quarter to six, he was brought to the room again. He didn't see Raven and her husband but was hoping that she'd be on time. Something else that he was going to make her do was to be on time in the future for meetings. He was never on time, but he was the boss, so it didn't matter all that much.

When the meeting was called to order, he still hadn't seen Raven. There were lots of people hanging around, and he ignored them for the most part. As they were taking their seats, a man took the chair next to his, and a woman sat on the other side. That was when it occurred to him that it was Raven and the man her supposed husband.

"Raven is supposed to sit next to me. It's to give me a clear shot at her while I'm talking." The man said he was lucky that she was there at all, much less sitting next to him. "But you don't understand. She's supposed to let me ask for forgiveness and give it to me because I had to take these classes. That's the way it's supposed to work."

"Well, you'll just have to be happy with it working this way. It's doubtful that she'll forgive you for your mistreatment of her, and she's staying as far from you as she can and still be in the classroom with you." He tried again to get the man to trade places with him, at least so that he was between them, and it wasn't going to happen. Raising his hand, he told the teacher how they were messing up the plans that had been set in place from the beginning, and she told him to go with the flow; it didn't matter where she was sitting, so long as she was there.

"But he said she's not going to forgive me." He found that he really wanted that too, to make sure that she was beholden to him for just a little while. "How am I supposed to work with this with so much negativity going on right now? I didn't plan on things going this way. I have to have her sitting next to me."

The teacher asked if he'd tried asking if he'd move, and the man simply said 'no'. Once it was established that he wasn't going to trade or move, Daniel felt his temper getting the better of him. The teacher was saying that he'd come so far that he should not let a little thing like setting arrangements get in the way.

"But it's not the way that I have dreamed of this day." He didn't like that he sounded whiny, but things weren't going his way. It was just a seat, he knew, but his temper was getting out of control until he had made himself slightly sick with it. "Make them trade places so that I can have it my way. Things will be just as I planned when things go my way."

"Daniel, you're being unreasonable. Just settle down and let the two of them sit where they want. It's not going to be that big of a deal after you tell her what you've been practicing to tell her." Even the teacher, he never knew her name, even if he'd been told it, was getting frustrated with the way things were going. "You start. Just tell her what you planned on telling her when you saw her again. And remember, this is your final meeting with us if things go well."

"This is just unreasonable. I can't tell her what I've been planning because she's not close enough for me to pop in the mouth if she gets lippy with me." Everyone turned to look at him. "Oh, like you care about how I conduct myself. None of you are going to get your jobs back for very long because you can't hide your temper like I can."

On some level, he knew that he was messing things up, but he couldn't stop now. When the man sitting next to him stood, so did Raven. He thought for sure that he'd got his way and smiled at them when suddenly they were at the door to leave. If they left, he was going to be in this stupid class for another six weeks, and he'd not get his job back until he had finished them. Standing up, he went to the door with them and decided to talk to the man.

"How are you going to make it if she's not working for me? You're not, that's how, and her stupid idea of going to college is just that, stupid. There is no way that the two of you are going to be able to afford the house you purchased with her going to 'college' to be an attorney. She's not all that smart anyway." He looked around the room when someone said his name. "I'm working right now. Just give me a few minutes to get things straightened out with her husband, and things will be back to normal. No man wants to see his wife wasting money on things like higher education when she should be working a good job for me."

"She's not going to be working for you anyhow, nor anyway. Even if we did need the money, which we do not. And if you don't step back a few steps, I'm going to hit you again, and this time you won't be so quick to have hospital care. You'll be in the mortuary where you should have been put the first time I had anything to do with you." The anger in his voice surpassed even his, and he did take a couple of steps back. But then he remembered who he was and where all this was going, and he drew back his fist to hit Raven.

She was the cause of all of them, and it was time

that she realized he wasn't one to mess with. His fist never got close enough for him to brush her hair away before his arm was up behind his back, and he was screaming in pain.

"What are you doing? I was going to make her see reason. No woman, especially not her, should ignore me when I have something to impart. Let me go." He heard the pop in his arm, and the feeling of needing to throw up had him gagging. "I'm sick. You've broken me, and I demand that you let me go."

He had no idea who was holding him, and he couldn't make himself turn enough to see who it was. Just as he was feeling like he might pass out from the pain, he was jerked again, and that was it. His body just fell into itself, and he was out.

Chapter 3

Cassian needed to cool his temper, and standing around waiting on the police to handle things was making even his dragon pissy with him. He wanted blood, and he needed to protect his — Raven put her smaller hand into his, and all his anger just went away. He stood there staring at her while the others were talking about how Daniel Winters was going to be put back in jail and made to retake the classes that he'd only just failed.

"I thought he was doing much better." Maria Santos, the teacher of the class, grabbed Daniel by the arm when it was apparent that he was going to hurt Raven. "You can bet this is going to look bad to his company. To think that all this time he was playing at me to get me to let him — what did he say he was going to do? Pop her a few times? I should have done something sooner rather than when he was ready to hit her. For that, I apologize profusely."

"You think they'll let him have his job back after trying to hurt me again?" Raven never let go of his hand, for which he was grateful. She had calmed him and his beast, and he couldn't have been more in love with her.

There is no telling what would have happened had she not touched him when she had. There wouldn't have been a building left had she not, he knew that for sure. "I don't think I'd go into a restaurant that would hire someone like him back after twice now that he's tried to kill me."

"I'm going to recommend just that. That they don't hire him back for the reason that he has not learning anything from these classes." Maria looked so distressed that he found himself wanting to comfort her and tell her that it wasn't her fault. It was something that he saw in Daniel's head just as they were pulling up to the front of the police station, where the meeting was going to be held. "He certainly had me fooled. And I'm not easily fooled."

Cassian thought that she wanted people to learn the lessons that she was teaching, and she saw what she wanted to when asking them the questions at the end of each class. Daniel had been threatening Raven in his mind from the very beginning, and she'd chosen not to see it. But she did now, and he supposed that was all that mattered.

After Daniel was taken away in an ambulance, things started to settle down. The others in the classroom were doing what needed to be done about their asking for forgiveness for those that they hurt, and he and Raven left early. She was still shaken up a bit, but seemed to be holding onto her tears until they were alone. Not that he blamed her, she'd been hurt enough today, and no one had touched her. As soon as they were in the car, headed home, she put her hand on his as he was putting the car into gear to drive.

"Would you have killed him?" He didn't hesitate but said that he would have if not for her. "Believe it or not, I wanted you to kill him, but I knew that wouldn't have worked out well for either of us. So when I touched your hand in mine, it was like a calmness rolled over me, unlike anything I've ever felt before. If I didn't believe that you're my mate before, I do now."

"I'm glad for us both." He kissed her on the mouth and put the car in reverse. As he was backing up, he realized something else. She trusted him to not harm her either. And he might well have, being that she was so close to him, when he'd been ready to shift. He would have hurt a great many people had he shifted then to just take out the one man.

The rest of the ride home was done in silence. Both of them had a great deal on their mind; he knew that he did, and he wanted to sort through his emotions before he got angry again. He knew too that if Daniel had touched Raven, he would have ripped his throat out and killed him on the spot.

Once they were in the house, she went to the dining room. The view from that room could calm him down, too, when he was having a bad day. Something about the roses and other mid-blooming flowers had him sitting in the room for hours on end just watching the other creatures in the back yard. It was much like it was in the other realm, too, where things just seemed to have a calming effect on him, no matter how he was feeling.

Sitting down at his desk, he was glad to have something to do that would occupy his mind. So long as he was totally focused on the paperwork in front of him, he could get things done. Just so he didn't think about the meeting today or the outcome of it. His phone ringing had him answering with a short, curt saying of his last name.

"Is this Cassian Savage?" He asked who was calling. "I have been trying to reach out to Raven Savage for days now. She sent in an application for admittance to our fine university a few weeks ago, and I wanted to personally congratulate her for making the cut." He asked him to hold on while he got her. And just like he thought, she was enjoying the backyard, over thinking about what had happened today. The smile on her face told him it all.

He handed her the phone and stood there waiting for her to get off before he left. He told himself that it was so that he could get the phone back from her, but it was more than that. He wanted to see her happy about the news that she was getting so that he could celebrate with her. He could see on her face just when she'd been told that she was going to be able to go to the academia that she'd chosen for her extended classes.

"I got into the campus that I wanted." He danced a little jig with her around the dining room and laughed when she did. It was wonderful news, and he was glad that he got to share it with her. "I have six weeks to get ready for fall classes. Are you sure that we can afford it? I don't want to have to work, but I will if we need the money."

"No, you don't ever need to work. I've told you that before." He was so happy for her that he pulled her into his arms. "This will be epic for us. You'll be going to classes, and I'm going to be a house husband to keep the home fires burning. I know you'll be the most brilliant attorney ever made. Let's go and celebrate tonight. Dinner and a movie. We'll have to make up time for us to be together, too, before you get your classes set up. Just so we have plenty of time to continue getting to know each other."

"I love that idea." He found that he didn't want to pull away, and she didn't seem to want to either. "Would you like to invite your family to come along? They have been very helpful in getting me into the college that I wanted to be in."

"Tonight is just for you." He nodded after smiling down at her. "I've been waiting on some good news for today, and this is it. It's turned into a wonderful day today, and I'm so happy that we get to share it."

"You make me happy." He watched her face when she frowned. "I think that I'm in love with you. Isn't that the strangest thing? I never thought that it would happen for the two of us. I keep waiting for you to tell me that you don't really like me and can't wait to get rid of me."

"Never would I feel that way about you." She put her hands on his shoulders as he lowered his head towards hers. "I would love to kiss you right now. Tell me no before it's too late, and I'll back away."

When she didn't say anything, he lowered his head until his lips were touching hers. Even her breath tasted good to him, and he couldn't wait to savor all of her. Brushing his lips over hers, he deepened the kiss so that he could taste what she was offering.

Cassian tried his best not to overwhelm her by taking too much. When she stepped forward, putting one of her legs between his, it was all he could do not to shout to the world that she was his mate. And that she loved him. As he deepened the kiss even more, he moved her so that her breasts were crushed against his chest, and he could feel the moment that her nipples hardened. Moving her mouth more in line with his own, he felt the moment that she was surrendering to him, and he couldn't believe his luck. But he also didn't want to overwhelm her too much, so he pulled back. Her small whimper made him kiss her once more before he stood there holding onto her. Her eyes were still closed, and she held onto his arms like he was a lifeline to her. He could only hope that he was, just for her.

"Raven?" Her whispered name had her looking up at him. "We're going to be caught here in the hall if we take this any further. She looked slightly confused and staggered just a little when she took a step back. "Careful, love. I can't let anything happen to you right now. Let me help you to the couch."

Once she was sitting on the couch, she seemed to understand why she'd been moved. He didn't get up and move from her when it was obvious she was embarrassed; he simply held her hand while she looked around the room, any place but where he was sitting. When she seemed to get her bearings right, she looked at him and smiled.

"I got caught up in the moment." He told her that he had as well. And that he'd like more of those moments to get lost in. "I would as well. But not right now. I want you, obviously, but I don't know that I'm ready for that part of our relationship just yet."

"So long as you're telling me that you're not opposed to us being together, I'm fine with waiting on you to come to me." She smiled even bigger, and he couldn't help himself; he smiled back at her. She was his everything. "We're getting along nicely, and I don't want you to back away from me now that we have this between us."

"Yes, I understand." She stood up, and he let her. If he had been honest with her about how painfully hard his cock was, it might well have had her back off more. Instead, she said she was going to the dining room again and would enjoy the afternoon. He sat there until he could get up without hurting himself to go back to his office. He was sure he'd get nothing done, but he was going to give it his best shot at getting work finished up for the day.

It was nearly four when he finally got things squared away on his desk. There hadn't been that much, not enough to keep his mind from wandering, but he finally made himself concentrate, and it was finished up in no time. Putting the paperwork away, he was about as ready for the rest of the evening to celebrate with his mate. It wasn't every day that someone he knew got accepted into a good college.

He knew that Raven was getting ready in her bedroom, and he took the stairs two at a time to go to his room. He hoped that it wouldn't be long before they were sharing a room, but he wasn't going to rush things. She was happy, and he was happy with the way that things were going. All they needed was for her to trust him a bit more, and things would be where they should be. Even if he had to wait for months or years, he would do so because he loved her and she loved him.

After putting on a suit and tie, he made the reservations at one of his favorite places to eat. When he'd asked her where she wanted to go, she told him that she didn't get to go out all that often but hoped the place would have cloth napkins. That was something that he could work with, and got the last table when he called. They had about everything on the menu from seafood to steaks and everything in between, so he hoped she'd be able to find herself something to eat.

The movie that he got tickets for was easy enough too, as she'd been telling him about the new movie that was coming out and how much she wanted to see it. He knew nothing about the movie but was happy to be hanging out with her, so he didn't even look up reviews about the thing, so he'd not know the plot. He couldn't remember the last time he'd been to the movies and was glad that she had agreed.

While waiting for her in the hallway, he wished he'd gotten her some flowers. There were plenty on the stand with the vase on it in front of him, but he would have felt foolish had she caught him taking flowers from there for her. In the last moment, he did pick one off for his lapel and put it in the button hole. He was about as ready as he'd ever been. Then she came down the stairs.

"Christ, you're more beautiful than I remember you ever being." The dress, what he could see of it, was royal blue and matched his tie. Her cape was midnight black, and it looked delicious as it wound around her ankles. Even the little bits of peeking of her shoulders that he saw when she was coming down the stairs didn't help his imagination at all. All he could see was the dress and cape on the floor next to the bed, and the two of them tangled in the sheets. "I might well be immortal, but you're testing me right now. You look good enough to eat."

~*~

When they got to the restaurant, a place she'd only dreamed of being able to go someday, she took off her cape so that she could watch his face when she showed off to him. She'd been thinking of wearing a dress like this one for weeks now and was glad that she'd been able to surprise him with it. The low-cut front and back were more than she could have hoped for in a dress for going out to dinner with Cassian.

For the entire dinner, he kept staring at her. He was also touching her in intimate ways that had her hair stand up on her arms and neck. Nothing could have prepared her for the looks that he gave her, which seemed to be filled with hope and lust. Both feelings she could understand as she was having the same.

Raven was trying to find a comfortable way to sit by squirming around on the hard surface, but until he put his hand over hers, she thought she was hiding her pain pretty well. Her pussy was weeping and felt swollen. Like she was in need of something more, but it wasn't working out for her. However, the strangled look on Cassian's face made her realize that she was only making it worse and stopped moving.

"If you don't sit still, we're never going to be able to come back here again. I'm going to strip you down right now and have my way with you. I can smell you, and you're driving both me and my dragon crazy." He let her hand go and smiled at her. It was a painful look that he had on his face, and she had to swallow a laugh, if not for the same pain she was in. "Thank you. Let's just enjoy our meal."

For the rest of the meal, everything was a blur. She knew that she had ordered and had eaten, but she'd been surprised by her empty dinner plate being taken away. There was mention of dessert, but if she had any, she had no idea. As soon as Cassian paid the check, they were out the door and to the car in record time. She felt like a puppet on a string and could only move when Cassian guided her around.

As soon as they were out of the restaurant, he was nearly dragging her to the car. As soon as she was pressed against the hard surface, she moaned. If Cassian had done it to her, she wasn't sure, but it was the most delicious feeling that she'd ever felt. His cock was grinding into her pussy like he was fucking her, and she came twice before she could beg him for more.

The cool breeze over her breasts was momentary,

then she felt the wet heat of his mouth. As he suckled at her breasts, she held him to her until she was dizzy with need. Riding him, his hard cock right there where she could feel it, she gave herself two more heady climaxes as he feasted on her neck and throat.

"I'm not going to make it home." She didn't want him to. If he took her right now, here in the open like they were, she knew that she'd come hard and probably pass out. She was so needy that she was sure that if Cassian felt half as needy as she did, he was in a great deal of pain. That was when she felt his bare cock on her thigh and nearly sobbed with relief. "Try not to scream, and I'll do the same."

He entered her. There was no buildup or him using any foreplay, though she thought that their entire evening had been foreplay. As soon as she was filled with his cock, she came hard enough that she bit her lip hard enough to draw blood. Everything after that seemed to go from climax to climax until she was simply too weak to go on. But Cassian was still fucking her, and she knew on some level she was going to be sore tomorrow.

Holding onto him tightly, she wrapped her legs around his hips and held him to her. As soon as he licked her throat, she knew that he was going to bite her, and that would be the end of her being conscious. As soon as he sank his teeth into her flesh, she screamed out loud at the pain/pleasure of it all and felt her eyes roll to the back of her head.

When she woke, she was still being held by Cassian, and he was cursing. She didn't know what had happened in the few seconds she'd been out, but it had her laughing. When he looked down at her, she asked him what had happened, and he chuckled a bit.

"You were supposed to be quiet." She said he was just too good. "Thank you, but I fear we're going to have company soon and should be dressed when they get here. I love you."

"And I love you. With all that I am." She helped him with his clothing as she straightened up her own. There really wasn't too much to her dress. It had a long slit up the leg that was now longer. Even the top that had just hung around her neck was torn, and she had to smile. "I didn't even know that you tore this up. I can just put on something different. What would you like me to be wearing?"

"Nothing at all." That made her laugh all the harder, and she was still thinking of something to wear when someone came up from behind Cassian. "Can I help you?"

"We heard screams. Did you?" Cassian said that he'd heard them but thought it was just a couple of cats. "I don't know. It sounded like someone was in a great deal of pain. Are you two all right?"

"Just fine. We're both just getting ready to go home." The man looked like he wanted to detain them more, but there really wasn't much he could do about it. As she was let into her side of the car, she had finally settled on a pair of nice slacks and a pretty blouse. Her body was suddenly chilled in the night air. She noticed that Cassian had on a pair of jeans and a dress shirt with a tie. They just looked like a normal couple coming out of a restaurant. "I think you'll find that it was just a couple of stray cats out for a good time. That's what I heard anyway."

When he got in the car and started the engine, she asked him if he'd just called her a stray cat. He was laughing so hard that he could barely drive and sat in their parking space for an extra few minutes until he got himself under control. She joined him as it was quite funny.

The drive home was made mostly in silence. She started to get sore and reached up to touch the place on her neck where he'd bitten her. He asked her if she was all right, and she told him she was better than all right, she was fucking fantastic.

"I'm sorry about the way that I took you." She said that she enjoyed it as well. "I know you did, but it was dangerous for us to have had sex right out there in the open like we did."

"No harm done. I'm glad that we were able to get to know one another in that way. Even though I sounded like a cat in heat." He laughed again, and she joined him. There was something so boyishly charming about Cassian right now, and she fell in love with him more. "I have to admit that I can't wait to get home and into something more comfy. Like our bed. You will sleep with me tonight, won't you?"

"Of course. I'd love that. I don't know that I could be another moment away from you now that I've tasted paradise." When he took her hand into his and kissed the back of it, she felt like she could conquer the world. She never realized that he was a romantic until just then. "I will sleep better tonight. I'm not going to have to take any cold showers before going to bed. It's difficult to get warmed up very well after that."

"I'm sorry. I was so afraid that you'd realize that I wasn't for you or something. I guess it could still happen, but I'm not nearly as afraid of it as I was. I guess when you tell me that you love me, I believe you now." She thought about what she'd said. "I know now that you'd not lie to me about something so important as love. I've never been in love before."

"Me either. It's a heady feeling, don't you think?" She nodded, then remembered that he couldn't see her, so she told him it was. "I can't wait to have you in my arms through the night now. Just to be able to hold you will be more than my heart can take at the moment."

They didn't talk much more. Only remembering that they both had things to do in the morning kept her mind on the tasks that she had to get finished before starting college in a few more weeks. If she was honest with herself, she was nervous about starting something so daunting, but she knew that with the support of the Savage family, she'd be all right. They were the best family a woman could hope for.

As soon as they were home, a wonderful name for a place that they both loved, she made her way up to the bedroom. Needing a shower, she knew that she could work out the kinks in her body that way, and she'd feel better in the morning. Almost as soon as she was under the spray of hot water, Cassian joined her.

They only touched and massaged each other rather than having shower sex. She wasn't really in the mood right now as she was exhausted all of a sudden, but Cassian seemed to understand. After scrubbing her back for her, she did the same for him. It was a nice way to end the evening, and she was profoundly happy that she'd finally gotten over her fear of him leaving her.

She rarely woke in the middle of the night, but tonight she woke at around two. The room was warm, and she snuggled down deeper under the covers until she realized that she needed to go to the bathroom. Getting up, she was alarmed to find someone in the bed beside her until she realized that it was Cassian. He tried his best to keep her in the bed with him, but she finally won out. Rushing to the bathroom and then washing her hands, she was back in bed in no time and again snuggled under the covers with Cassian, holding her.

The room was flooded with light when she got up again. This time, she took her time getting to the bathroom because the room was cooler, and she didn't have to go to the bathroom as badly as she had earlier. Just as she was thinking about taking another shower, she turned to find Cassian in the room with her. His smile was like a beacon that lit up her morning. Kissing and hugging him, the two of them took another shower together before heading down to the kitchen to get themselves something to eat.

It was well after noon when she finished up her tasks for the day. She'd had to order a laptop, something that the university required her to have, and Ace was more than happy to help her get the best one. He and Tank were going out today to try and find a place to have a computer store put in, and he'd been doing his research about computers so he could have a conversation with the man about computers if it came to that.

The rest of her afternoon was spent with Ace and Tank. She loved these two cousins, and they seemed to really like her. After spending the afternoon with them, she had just enough time to get herself together for Cassian when he came home. He'd been working with Tucker and the others all day on two projects that were near to their hearts. One of them was the school buildings. The other was the new rec center that was going to be put in place of the old school buildings, so that it would be a place where the kids could meet up after classes and hang out.

She knew that the school buildings were starting to show some wear and tear on them. They'd been built in the latter part of the century and were not as up to date as they'd like them to be. The air conditioners and furnaces needed repair, and there wasn't enough room in the cafeteria to serve as many students at one time. The classes were getting bigger, and the rooms were still the same. It made for some of the kids not getting the attention that they might well need because of the overcrowding. Teachers didn't much care for it either, and they wanted everyone to be happy about teaching and going to school around here.

It amazed her that so much could change in just twenty years with buildings. Especially ones that were being used daily by hundreds of people—big or small. It just being outdated with the amount of electrical things like outlets and internet services was enough to boggle the mind. But there were things like upgrades made by the state that were also needed.

There were grants they could use for the school that would get them new buildings, as well as follow the updates that were mandated for the new buildings. The tax levy had passed for the new school, and they were excited to be able to take on this project for the area. It was going to be great for the kids coming in the fall next year to be able to start fresh. She was excited too, for when her own children started school in the district.

Chapter 4

Cassian wasn't sure what to make of the email from one of his buddies from long ago. Something about coming to visit the town before it was torn down. After calling and having to leave a message for Harlin, he decided to go and find Raven to see if she was up to anything. They'd been making love every morning and night since they went out to eat that one time.

"I have some things I need to ask you about. I can test out of some life classes, but I need a proctor who's not related to me. I don't know anyone who isn't related to me." He told her that he didn't think that any of the cousins were her cousins. "Well, that's just mean. I love them like they're my brothers, and now I find out that we're not related at all? But I guess that's all right. I can use one of them to help me out with some of the classes that I can opt out of."

She decided on Ace since he wasn't her cousin, and being mayor of their town would hold a lot more weight than anyone else would. She had to take four tests over the next five days in order to opt out of seven of her classes for this semester. Raven was very happy about that. But only if she passed them. Cassian knew she could do it.

She was planning on taking a full load of classes so that she could finish in a reasonable amount of time. It wasn't as if she didn't have plenty of time to become an attorney, but she wasn't used to being immortal yet, and he knew she'd be able to live out her life without hurrying through things when she lived a few hundred years. He knew that he'd wanted to do everything quickly so he could learn different trades, but that hadn't worked out so well when he got bored with life. If Raven hadn't come along when she did, he didn't want to think about how bored he'd be right now without his mate. She was brightening up his life like nothing had ever done before.

When she left to talk to Ace, he decided to finish up on the paperwork that he'd been putting off in favor of hanging out with Raven. It didn't take him long to get it finished up just as his phone was ringing. It was his old buddy and dragon friend, Harlin Spelling.

"I got your message, but I don't understand it. We're putting in new schools around here, as well as a rec center. If we're not going to be a town anymore, no one bothered to tell me about it." He said that he'd heard that the mayor had been run out of town and that he was being usurped by some animal. "Nothing like that happened. We do have a new mayor, but he's been getting things fixed up at a fanatical rate. What made you think that?"

"I don't know why, but I figured it was you guys having the town put to dirt because they weren't playing ball with you. Isn't that what happened to the other town that you lived in? They forever had their hands out wanting something done, and you just got tired of it? I heard that they've been closed down as a city and can't even get mail delivered, as the post office was shut down about ten years ago. I guess there are a few people still living there, but they're not doing much in the way of trying to save the town."

"You should come by and see what our cousin has been up to. If there is a grant or a federally subsidized loan that he can use, he's been right on top of it. In addition to the new schools being built this spring and into summer, we have just about all new sidewalks, and the pool is being redone as well. It looks like a new town around here." He told him he might just take him up on it. "I'll tell my new mate."

"You have a mate? Why didn't you start with that? Congratulations on her finding you. Christ, it's been so many years since my own mate has passed that I nearly forgot that there are still some dragons out there that are still looking." He told him how Tucker and Kings had found them as well. "What is this world coming to, I ask you? I'm glad to hear that Tucker isn't going by Savage anymore. I always felt sorry for him when we were growing up. He just seemed so down all the time."

Tucker didn't even know that he had a first name other than being called Savage by his family. When one of the others pointed out that his first name was Tucker, he'd been about as shocked as he'd been in finding a mate after all this time. Of course, it helped him too that Kaida called him that, along with the others who were around now. Tucker had had a horrific life before his parents were all murdered by Margo, his sister, and he felt bad for the older dragon about it, too. Not that his nor Brenin's life had been all that different. It seemed to him that they heard that their last name was Savage and took it to heart, treating everyone around them like the name implied.

Now that they were all dead, they all had a better life. They certainly were richer in their friendship with each other. It had always amazed him how much his parents had always hated the other cousins, especially Tucker. That had always surprised him in how much hatred they'd had for the sweetest guy he knew. Well, he was sweet now, thanks to Kaida. She made them all want to be better men.

After talking with Harlin and inviting him to come and stay with them, he felt better. He was going to remember the story about the town to tell Ace the next time he saw him. It was funny to him that people would make up stories like that and expect no one would check on them. It would have been bad for them to get businesses to come around if they thought that the town was going down the tubes.

He knew that Harlin would make sure that it got around that the town wasn't in trouble and tell people that he knew it was being updated all over the little burg. He was especially excited about the sidewalks being fixed. They were a danger all on their own. But Ace, true to his word to the people who had voted for him, had gotten them fixed with little to no fuss at all.

Walking over to see him now, he kissed Raven when he saw her first. Her cheeks were all flushed like she was happy, and it made him feel really good. He didn't know why he wasn't jealous about her spending time with his cousins, and he was for everyone else. Especially Daniel Winters.

Daniel had knocked her around on her last day of work and had been arrested again. And since he'd failed his anger management classes, he no longer had a job to go to. Right now, he was sitting in jail waiting for his trial for causing a scene in the class. There was also another hearing going on for the Connors and Waggoner about the kidnapping and murder of Trevor's family when he was about one year old.

They were only going to be sentenced at the second, three people to see when they were going to prison and for how long. He figured that Jason Waggoner would get several life sentences, as he had confessed to killing as many as fifty people when he'd been free. That was another guy that he wanted off the streets. He'd been causing Skye to have nightmares of him getting loose and hurting her again since he'd been arrested. His heart broke for the other woman.

Ace wasn't busy when he was talking to him, but he did have the specs on the new computer company that they were hoping would come to their town. As it was now, they had to travel all the way to Zanesville, about a twenty-minute drive, to get anything fixed up when it came to cell phones and computers alike. Having one in their own town was going to be epic, not to mention nice to have, so that when the schools had trouble with their setup, it could be dealt with quickly. They didn't have a lot of trouble, at least he didn't think they would when they started out at the new buildings. That was another thing that would be updated when they built new classrooms: all the computer equipment for the classrooms.

"I talked to him for about three hours. He wants to start out large and then have room to expand when he wants. I think he has some good ideas about his shop. He wants to be able to repair computers and resell them to some of the customers who might not be able to afford up-to-date computer systems. Also, he'll have a showroom where he can show off the newest computer systems. Raven got a good deal on the laptop that she needed for classes, as he gives a discount on the ones that are purchased just for school. She was excited." He told him that she was downloading the links on it so that she would have the books that she needed before classes started. "I heard that teachers are doing that. You pay for a book online so that it's nothing you have to carry around with you. Brilliant idea if you ask me." He then told him about the story of the town being demolished.

"He said that he'd take care that the people who told him about it knew the true story. I thought it would hurt us with new businesses coming around to see if they want to build here or not." Ace said that it might well have. "I also thought that we could be a good town for others needing help with getting things around town done, like the pool and the sidewalks. You'll probably be getting calls from people to see what it is that you've done. It could be a good feather in your cap when it comes to reelection time again."

"I'm having fun right now, but I'm sure that once things are finished being repaired or replaced, I'm going to have nothing to do but walk around town shaking hands and kissing babies. Do men do that anymore?" Cassian said it sounded dangerous to him, what with all the rules regarding safe distances and other rules that people have. "Yeah, you're probably right. I'd hate to have my head bashed in for trying to kiss a kid who has a cold or something. I can't catch whatever is wrong with them, but it's still nasty to think about."

They talked about some of the other things

that were going on around town. The pool would be finished by next spring. Even though it looked like it might not ever be finished, he could see that the holes were being planned out and things like rebar for the walls were coming into the town via the trucks he'd seen around the area.

The pool was going to be twice as big as it had been, and there was going to be lift equipment for the handicapped who wanted to use the pool, too. The lift was what started the whole thing about Ace becoming mayor. He'd found enough money without raising taxes to get the job done for nothing to the townspeople. The only thing they were paying for was the renovation of the pool itself, and most were excited about that. It would certainly be more room for those who wanted to use the pool in the summer.

"I have two more businesses that are thinking of coming here. One of them will take over the old building out on Route Sixty where the old basket plants used to be. It would be fifty-five more jobs for the people around here, and that would be great. Because the building was meant to make baskets, it had a lot of open spaces around that could be used for just about anything. And that would save them time and money when moving in." He asked about the other business. "It's a business that trains people on how to use a sewing machine. And the products that they sell will be made locally. I'm very excited about that one because there are a lot of people who would be good at that. He said that he trains women who are going back into the workforce after so long and just need to update their resumes. I'm not sure on all the ins and outs, but we're just in the talking stages of having them put their plant here."

The four of them talked about getting dinner. Ace was all for it, but his brother was going out on a date tonight. Good for him was all he could think about, as before meeting Raven, he'd not been out on a date in a long time. Sometimes they would hear the name Savage and would immediately think of money. He had some, but he wasn't going to give it away on some date that he'd had with a human. Then he remembered that his mate was human and decided that he'd keep his opinions to himself from now on. It might well get him in trouble at home if he didn't.

They decided to go out somewhere fancy for dinner. Not super fancy, but some cloth napkins as well as a wine list. It wouldn't get them drunk at all, but it was nice to get a little buzz off of drinking it. He was also fond of a beer with his pizza for the same reason.

Dinner was nice, as it was wonderful conversations too. They talked about the new schools as well as the new pharmacy that was coming to town. The one that had been in town until recently had been purchased by some larger group, and they had decided to close it down. It had been difficult for the people around town to get their medications, especially those who didn't drive and had been dependent on the local pharmacy that had been in town. It also sold school supplies in the school year, which would be good for last-minute projects for students.

~*~

Raven was reading one of her college texts the next morning when she was called to the station house by one of the officers. Apparently, Daniel wanted to talk to her, and she was debating whether to go. He was a pain in the ass, and if she could talk to him where he couldn't get to her, she'd be fine with that. The man wanted to knock her around something terrible, and she didn't like him all that much.

Walking to the stationhouse, she was there in just a few minutes. Her plan was to go to the library when she was finished so that she'd have something to read other than school books for the rest of the summer. When she got to the stationhouse, she couldn't believe how calm they all looked, probably from living in a small town where they had very little crime and not much to do. She was asked to leave her purse and sweater behind in the event that he would grab them to get to her. Anything to keep her safe. She'd also told Cassian what she was doing in case things got out of hand. She didn't think that it would; he was in jail after all, with armed men.

"*Just make sure that you don't sit close enough to him so that he can touch you.*" She said she was going to do that so that he'd not hurt her. "*If he does, the entire department will be gone. I won't hold back if they let you get hurt.*"

"*Surely you don't mean that.*" When he didn't say anything, she changed the subject. "*My classes start in just two weeks. I'm so excited about them that I could bust.*"

"*I can tell. I'm glad to be able to be around when you need help, too. It might well have been a long time since I was a practicing attorney, but I remember enough to keep me and the rest of us out of hot water all the time.*" She asked him if she'd be able to help them out as well. "*I don't see why not. You'll have fresh eyes on things, and that will be helpful in all kinds of situations. Plus, I think that you'll be more up to date on laws than I am right now. I know nothing about cybercrimes that would be helpful. I have read about it, but I didn't take any classes that would have me knowing what sort of laws are being broken.*"

"*I'm taking a lot of classes that have to do with that. I guess with everyone on computers anymore, there is a great deal of that going on.*" He told her how he'd read a few articles on the subject and was worried about it. "*There is a great deal to be worried about, too, from what I read. Identity theft is the worst. People aren't being as secure as they should be when it comes to putting their information out there.*"

She was waiting for Daniel to be brought to her

in a special room. The officer who was in the room with her assured her that he wasn't going to be leaving her alone with the other man. She was glad for that. She didn't trust Daniel any further than she could spit, and that wasn't all that far. As soon as he was brought into her room, he was chained not just to the floor but to the table as well. The officer told him to stretch out his arms so that she could see how much room she had before he could touch her. Her idea was not to put her hands on the table at all and scooted her chair back so she'd not be tempted.

"I have to go. Daniel is here, and he looks like someone has taken a stick to his face and hands. I hope he's getting his comeuppance while in here so that maybe he'll be a nicer man when he's let out." Cassian laughed, and she could feel his supposed humor about that statement. *"Yeah, I don't believe it either. Later. I love you."*

He told her that he loved her as well and would be there if she needed him. She hoped that she wouldn't, but she didn't know what to do if he were to touch her. She had it in her head to tempt him to see what the other officer would do to him, but decided against that. There was no point in poking the bear, as her grannie was so fond of saying.

"What do you want with me? I think I've made it perfectly clear that I want nothing to do with you." He said that she needed to get him out of jail by not pressing charges again. "I'm not going to do that.

Believe it or not, I like you being behind bars. I do sleep better at night."

"I don't care what you want. It's been driving me crazy here because there is nothing for me to do. And now I just found out that I've lost my job because of you." She asked him how it was her fault that he'd lost his job. "Because if you would have just stayed clocked in and working for me that day, then none of this would have happened. I bet your husband regrets marrying you; you're so stubborn."

"He actually gives me whatever I want when I ask for it." He snorted like he didn't believe her. "What did you want so that I can tell you no again and go home. I have classes starting soon, and I have to get onto reading some of the books that I have."

"You can't seriously still be thinking about going to college. You're not smart enough to get into one, much less have the intellect to pass any of the courses." She thanked him. "You're welcome."

"It wasn't meant as a real thank you. I was being sarcastic with you." He told her he never understood that. "Whatever. It doesn't matter. What else did you want from me so that I can get on with my life? I heard that your trial is set for next month sometime and that you might well get a prison sentence for your violent acts against me."

"You haven't seen any violent acts against you, but you will once I get out of here." She said she wasn't worried about him, but in truth, she really was. Shivering slightly, she told him that she was done messing with him and was going to go home. She had better things to do than hang out with him. "You'll stay until I get what I want from you. You're going to stop pressing charges against me and get me out of here so that I can get my job back, and you'll work for me again. If you would just allow me to knock you around, I would be able to get all my frustrations out on you, and the rest of the staff will be happy for it. Otherwise, when I work again, there is no telling what will happen to the others that work for me if you're not there to cut them some slack."

"Let me get this straight. You want me to let you beat me up all the time just so the other staff will be safe from harm. That's not going to happen. First of all, I no longer work for you or the company, and secondly, you're insane if you think that anyone would be all right with you beating up one of the people who worked for you." He told her that she was missing the point that others would be safe. "I don't care about the others if you think that I'm going to be all right with that." She thought of something. "You should bring up your plan with the judge when he gets around to seeing you. I'm betting that he isn't going to be pleased with it any more than I am. And I think it's a done deal about you not going back to work there. You'll have to find yourself someplace else to work out your plan.

But don't think that I'm going to follow you. I've got better things to do than to allow you to beat on me."

"You're still missing the point. You'll be saving a lot of workers from harm if you would just allow me to knock you around a bit. Some days it'll have to be worse than it was on the day of the great beating, but I'm sure we can work something out about that. Maybe I can only hit you on your body and not your face. That way you can still work and look good." She stood up to leave and nearly sat again when he told her, really, he snarled at her to sit her ass back down. Going to the door, he was still screaming at her for not listening to him when she was out the door and into the hallway. The officer who was waiting at the door assured her that she was going to be just fine.

"He wants to be able to knock me around as if I'm his play toy or something." He said that they'd heard what he said and that it had been recorded. "What sane person thinks that I'd be all right with him doing that to me and allow it to happen more than one day? No one that's who."

She made her way to the front desk of the station and told them not to call her again. She wasn't going to come down here and put up with him saying those kinds of things to her again. They told her that they'd thought that he was going to tell her how sorry he was, that's what he'd told them he was going to do. As she was leaving the stationhouse, she heard from Cassian.

"I can feel your anger all the way across town. What's happened?" She told him everything, including how everyone would be safe if she were to agree with what he wanted. She was still so mad that she wanted to go back in there and give him a piece of her mind, but she was fearful that he'd not understand and think that because she came back, she was all right with what he wanted to do. It was insane to think that anyone would be all right with that. *"I'll have a talk with him about manners."*

"You'll end up killing him, and while I will visit you, I don't want to have to visit you in prison. He's not going to listen, and I think he has a screw loose or something. There isn't any way that he's sane and thinking that I'd be all right with what he's saying." Cassian laughed, and she wanted to hit him, too, but he was too far away. *"I'm not in the mood for you to find humor in my situation. He really thinks that I should be all right with this."*

"I think you're right in telling him to say that to the judge. He might not think it's funny, but he will get a kick out of it being said. They might order tests to be done on him to see if he really is thinking that what he wants is going to happen. Lesser things have gotten people declared insane. I don't even understand how he thinks it's going to be all right with me. I think I've shown him enough that I have no patience with him."

"Maybe he needs a lesson in manners, as you said. I can think of a few of them that he's not gotten yet. Just to

think...I can't believe that he actually thinks that anyone would be all right with what he's saying. Then he tells me that he'll only hit my body and not my face like he's expecting me to run the register or something while being beaten to shit." She wasn't so much angry with the man, she was, but she was more shocked that he'd be thinking what he was thinking. People just didn't want to get beaten all the time, no matter how much it saved their fellow workers. She'd bet that anyone who worked there with her would be upset as well about the treatment of her. At least she hoped they would be. *"I need to let go of all this frustration. I was going to the library to get a book, but I'm fearful that I'll be just too pissy with them to get anything but arrested."*

"Just tell them what you told me about Daniel, and I'm sure they'd understand. He's a cracker short of some cheese." She burst out laughing, causing the men around her to turn to look at her. One of them even winked at her as if they understood that she was talking to someone else. *"I will go and talk to him. I promise not to kill him unless he forces my hand. And since I feel like I can handle him right now, I'll do it on the way home from working. I'm almost finished here anyway. You'll be happy to know that we have two buildings that are ready to be used for the computer company and another one for the shop that's coming in that sells candles. I don't know how well they'll do at first, but they said they understood that the town is in flux right now and depending on other businesses*

to come to town."

"*Hopefully, they'll be able to hang on until other businesses see that they're making a go of it and come to open up a shop too. I guess they're not hiring very many people either.*" He told her that they were saying five, but he didn't see that working out either. "*I feel better now. Just not talking about him for a few minutes has taken away some of my anger or whatever it is that I was feeling. Are you really going to go and talk to him?*"

"*I am. I would feel better if I could make it clear to him that I'm not going to tolerate him treating you the way that he has, either. I'm thinking that he won't understand that, but it'll be worth it to me to see how he reacts to my own kind of threats. I really think that he's off his rocker, babe, and that's why he feels like he can say those things to you. Like you said, no sane person would think those things, much less say them out loud.*" She said that she didn't know, but was glad for someone else to take over with him. Then she told him how she'd told the stationhouse not to call her anymore, she wasn't coming there to listen to him go on about shit anymore. "*Good. If they call asking you to come again, I'll instruct the household not to allow the calls to come into the house. The station can deal with him.*"

Going to the library, she was happy to find that they had some new authors' books on display so that people could check them out. She got herself two of them so that she could read one of them, but it turned out to be nothing that she wanted to read. She would also leave a review for them as she was in the habit of doing when she could. Good or bad, she knew that it helped other readers to understand what the book was about and whether or not they might enjoy it as well. She was on her way home when she saw that Cassian's car was in front of the police station. She wished that she could be there to hear what he had to say, but knew that she was feeling better now and didn't want to be angry again about him.

Chapter 5

Cassian was finding humor in what Daniel had said to Raven. It sounded to him as if the man was insane to think that things could go his way. But he was going to talk to him about his manners when he got to see him, and he was happy that the stationhouse wasn't all that busy, so that they could bring him into the little room he'd been in before. As soon as he was seated and chained up, Cassian popped him in the nose, having his head snap back and blood pour from his nose. Neither the cop nor he said anything when Daniel started screaming about the pain he was in.

"Shut up." His mouth closed so tightly that it was a wonder that he didn't bite his lip or his tongue in the process. "Now this is the way things are going to go from now on. You'll not talk to my wife again. Ever. She's not going to be working for you, even if you were to ever find a place that would hire you. You're not going to be beating people so that you can be in a better mood, too. That ship has sailed, and you're not going to be on it. Do you understand what it is that I'm saying to you?"

"You hit me." He asked if he wanted him to

hit him again, and sadly, he declined. "You can't just come in here and hit me. If I were unchained, I'd show you why you can't do that again."

"If they were to unchain you, you'd piss your pants if they were to allow us to have at it. I'd kill you before your first blow was sent." He lunged at him, and Cassian didn't move. "You're not all that badass. In fact, I'd say you're nothing but a school yard bully that thinks just because he can talk a big game that people should listen."

"I'm just lucky that I'm chained up." He didn't bother telling him he was right, as he told him once again, he wasn't to bother Raven. "I don't know why you care if she's getting beaten up or not. She'd have a job instead of going to college, which would be a total waste of time. She's pretty and all, but she doesn't have the smarts to make it through college, much less be an attorney like she said that she wants to be."

"What makes you think that we're poor?" He said that the entire town was poor, and he wondered if he'd taken a good look around. "I have, and I'm doing something about the projects that are going on with my money and that of the rest of my family. Have you ever heard of the Savages?"

"You mean that supposedly rich bunch of fuckers that think they own the town? Yeah, so what? You might be a Savage, but you're in no way related to them. I've met them all, and you aren't even a blip on their radar in the amount of money that they have." He said that they were all related. "Sure you are. If so, then what are you doing being married to Raven? She's not that good-looking, and she has nothing to her name but a job that she should have been fired from a long time ago."

"You mean like you have been. Well, I hate to burst your bubble, but she's my wife, and she wouldn't ever have to work again if she didn't want to. Not that I care if you believe me or not, but that's the truth." He wanted to hit the man again, but decided that he'd be pushing his luck with that. "Have you learned anything from talking to the two of us? Like we're not going to be putting up with your shit anymore?"

"It's just a little bit of knocking her around. I don't know why so many people have a problem with that. It's not like I would have to do it daily. I mean, I won't insist that she come in on her days off to allow me to knock her around." This time, he popped him twice in the face and watched as his nose started to bleed a great deal. "Stop hitting me. I don't like it."

"Yet you want to do it to my wife. That is sort of a double standard, don't you think? Maybe I'll hire you just so when you open your mouth to say something stupid, I can hit you a couple of times and feel better about myself." He said that he was thinking of this all wrong. That it wasn't about him being hit, but him saving the lives of the people that worked for him. "As my wife said to you, I don't care about the other people when you think that beating on her is going to be all right with either of us. I find her to be precious and the owner of my heart, so no one will get to her but through me. And I think I've already shown you how I'd treat you if you so much as look in her direction again."

"You think she's just going to be all right with you hitting me all the time? She won't. She's the type of person who would lay down her life for a stupid mutt that got hit by a car. She'll care about the other people the first time I have to hit one of them when I have a bad day. And who's to say that I'll have a bad day every day? I could just have them once or twice a week, and she'd be off the hook for me knocking her around. Come on, you know that she has a soft heart. There is no way that she would not want to save everyone who is working for me. That's another thing that she's going to do: get me my job back. And think about this, when they promote me for being such a good manager and I have my own district, she'll be promoted too, so that she can come along with me. That's a win-win for all of us."

He was getting angry with talking to the man. There was no getting through to him, and he had a feeling that he understood some of the frustration that Raven had had with him. The man really was inside to think that anyone in their right mind would be all right with his supposed treatment of Raven. The man needed to be taken to the woodshed. Then he thought that it wouldn't do any good, as the man really thought that he was right. Standing up, he was ready to wash his hands of the other man when he said something about needing the money again.

"I don't need the money, and even if we were living out of a cardboard box, there is no way that I'd allow you to treat my Raven like you think you were." He said it would be a lot of money, more than she was making now. "As I said, I'd not take money for her treatment like you want her to be for anything in this world."

As he went out of the station, several people stopped him to tell him that the times he'd hit the man wouldn't be saved. The recording would be just gone, and there would be no one to dispute his word. He knew that he loved the people who worked here, and this just went to prove to him that they had a good team working for the town. He was going to suggest that they get new uniforms because he did notice that theirs were looking a lot worn. Ace would be able to find some money for that, or he'd just fund it himself.

Driving home, he had to stop twice to stop himself from taking his anger out on other drivers. Like Raven, he wasn't so much angry as he was frustrated about the way things had gone. He thought that he'd go in and tell him how things were going to go, and he'd be agreeable. The man really did have some odd ideas about how people should be treated in the workplace. He could only hope that he shared his plan with the judge when he came to town again, just so he could see firsthand what they'd been dealing with.

As soon as he got back to his house, he looked for Raven. Finding her in the kitchen with the cook, he pulled her up from the chair and held her. When she wrapped her arms around him, like before, he felt all his anger just slip away. She was the best medicine that he'd ever had for calming him down. It didn't hurt, too, that he loved her with all he was.

"I take it things didn't go well with Daniel." He said that he didn't want to talk about him. "Okay. What did you want to talk about? Something to do with dinner? We're having salmon with asparagus and hollandaise sauce. Also, a nice salad that will be just plain lettuce, as we're having pie for dessert, and I want to save room for it."

"That sounds really good." He still didn't let go of her when she pulled back enough to look at his face. "I hit him three times and it still didn't rattle his brain around to thinking that what he was saying was going to be all right with me."

"I wish I could have hit him. I know that I'd feel better, but I was more afraid of him hitting me back, which kept me from doing it. What did he say when you hit him? I'm betting it had something to do with me being hit, not him." He said that is exactly what he said. "I figured as much. If he gets out, and I'm hopeful that he doesn't, I'm going to buy myself a gun so that I can kill him if he touches me again. Do you think that he'll be getting out soon?"

"No, I don't. He's going to say something to the judge about how he's going to keep you with him when he gets promoted, and that will be the end of him being free. Some of the things that came out of his mouth still frustrate me to no end. Why did he ever get hired if that's the way that he'd been thinking?" Raven told him that he'd never done that before until that last day. "You likely never told him no before, and that's what set him off."

"I didn't tell him no because he was fairly fair with his working with me. I'd do my job and ignore him for the most part. He would get testy at times, but I just wrote that off as him being stressed at his job. It's one of the reasons that I didn't take the position that he had. I didn't want the stress." He pulled away from her when their cook said that their salads were ready.

Since they'd been eating in the kitchen while living in the big house, he sat down next to Raven when the salads were set in front of them. He might be a meat-eater, but he really enjoyed a nice salad once in a while. Especially when there was a special dressing that was made from scratch. It was a nice apple vinegar dressing that complemented the greens very well.

They both enjoyed dinner very much, and he was glad that they ate in the kitchen instead of the big dining room, which was cold when there was no one else around. They were talking about having the entire family over soon, and cook told them to let her know so she'd be able to have enough for them to eat. She'd been here before when they were eating with them, so she knew that it required a great deal of food to fill everyone up. Just as he was going to the living room to unwind, Lady Earth came to visit him.

"I've finally figured out what gift I was going to give to my dragons, but I decided that I wanted to start with you." She looked at Raven when she spoke, and he wondered what it would be. "I have since taken away the pain that comes with getting the extra magic when you bond. I don't know why something so wonderful needed to be followed up with so much pain in the first place. Silly way to give the gift of magic to someone that I dearly love."

"I did wonder if I got any more magic from Cassian when we mated or bonded, whatever you called it." She said that she'd gotten a great deal of it from all of the family and that she was powerful in her own right. "Thank you, but I really didn't need any more. I barely use what I had before."

"You'll need the extra magic for what I have in mind for all of you. I think that it will make you all happy too." She asked her what it was going to be.

"Oh, I can't wait to tell you. It'll be such a wonderful gift for all that you've done for me in just being the dragons that I have come to depend on. It'll be the gift of dragons."

Raven looked at him, and he was just as confused as she looked. "I have my dragon. And other than Ace and Tank, we have been doing very well with them, too." She told him that he misunderstood. "Then please tell us. I'm excited to know what brought you to us tonight."

"I'm gifting all of you the ability to shift into dragons. And each mate that comes along afterwards will have the same gift." Cassian had to sit down. The thought of being able to fly with Raven was almost more than he could handle. "Do you understand now? I want all of you to be my dragons so that the sky can be filled with you all again."

~*~

Raven knew that they'd all come to their home for food. Every time they gathered, they got food and ate lots of it. She'd been amazed at the amount of food that they would order, but now, instead of thinking they ordered too much, she often wondered if they had ordered enough. They were big men, and they had the appetite to go with it.

Trying her best not to think about the news that the Lady Earth had brought with her, she organized the different foods with the restaurants so that by the time everyone had arrived, the food would already be there. She was getting good at calling different restaurants to get food from them enough to feed her family, and them to have enough left over to do business for the rest of the evening. It was a lot of work, but—she was going to be able to fly.

Shaking her head, she tried to tell herself not to think about what might happen. She said that she wanted to present it to all of them, and would they please invite everyone over so that she could. Lady Earth said that she'd been working on the magic all these last three weeks and thought that she had it finished. Thought was a big word to her. What if it didn't work? Or what if there was only enough magic for a couple of them to fly? She would give up her spot for Ace and Tank. They'd been the longest without being able to fly, and they deserved it. She looked up when someone touched her arm. It was Lady Earth.

"You are very good and unselfish to want them to have this." She said that it was only right that they should, since they'd been born into a dragon household, it only stood to reason that they get it first. "There will be plenty of magic to go around, my dear. And tonight you will be able to go into the dark sky with the rest of them and have fun. You will enjoy it, won't you?"

"Oh yes. I've thought of nothing else since you arrived." She said that she was thinking of the downside, too. "Yes, well, I'm not used to things going my way, and this is a biggy. Don't you believe that if there is only so much magic, it should go to Ace and Tank?"

"As I said, that is very unselfish of you. But know that they thought that the women of the family should have it before them as you're mates to the other dragons." She looked over to where the men were standing and thought they were the sweetest men she knew. "They're excited for you and the other women more than they think of themselves. The three of you, plus Ace and Tank, will be flying tonight, Raven."

She sounded so sure that she wanted to believe her. But things that you believed in rarely turned out the way that you wanted them to. She didn't mean to be so negative, but in her heart, she knew that things weren't going to work out. And she smiled to herself, thinking that she'd be all right with that too. Raven had never flown and wouldn't miss it like someone who'd had it taken away from them. And that's the way she felt about Ace and Tank. They'd been born into a dragon family and had their magic of flight taken from them. It wasn't fair. Not for them nor anyone who had been born the same way.

Tucker was the last to arrive as he'd had the furthest to come from. He'd been in Columbus, going over some of the contracts that had been given to him by one of the businesses that were thinking about coming to town. It must have gone well, as he was in such a good mood that it was infectious with the others around the room. After eating his fill, there was enough food, and they sat in the living room, and Lady Earth began talking.

"Since I've had so much help with my gardens this year, we're going to have a bumper crop of flowers and blooms. In addition to that, we're going to have a fresh group of faeries born to help out with the new flowers. I'm even able to plant two of my fields twice this year thanks to Kings and Skye. I've never been so relaxed as I have been knowing that most of the burden of keeping the little ones working has been taken care of. For that, I have a gift for all of you. The ability to shift into dragons."

The room was silent, but she could tell that there would be questions. When Skye stood up and headed for the door, Kings asked her where she was going. With a smile on her face, she told him she was going to go out into the yard and shift. The rest followed.

"I've never done this before. How do I shift?" It was Kings who told his mate how to shift. "So I just think of her, and then I'll just become a dragon? That sounds entirely too easy. Does it hurt at all?"

"No, never. It feels like you've been given a second life as a dragon." They all watched as she stood in the middle of the backyard with her eyes closed. "You should be able to see her when she's ready. Sometimes she'll leap at you, but since you've never done this before, she might be as shy about it as you are. Just give her a chance."

Walking off in the distance, Raven thought of her own dragon. Would she be red or blue? Not that she cared, but it would be nice to be able to do the same things as Cassian could. Then she saw her.

Stopping in mid-step, she looked at the beautiful dragon. When she snarled at her, Raven couldn't help it, she laughed. Then she whispered for her to come to her, and she felt the magic surround her. When she opened her eyes, she saw things from a different height and perspective. Things were...well, they were more.

"Christ, Raven, you're beautiful." She laughed again and turned her head to look at Cassian. "Just be careful of your tail. If you knock down any trees, it will be hard to explain to the insurance company that a large dragon did the damage. I can't believe how magnificent you are."

She knew that on some level, she couldn't fly until it was dark out. They never flew during the day for fear of scaring the townspeople. They knew that they were dragons, but they didn't push their luck with having them around them. It was better at night anyway; they could see better in the darkness than they could during the daylight hours.

"*I feel so free, like you said.*" He came to her slowly, cautioning her about her tail. "I'll be careful. I don't really have a lot of control over it, but I'm keeping it tucked under my body for now."

"I'm going to touch you to see if you're hot or not. I don't know any other way to tell what sort of dragon you are." His hand felt small against her face, and she leaned down to him carefully. He seemed so small to her at the moment, and she relished the fact that he was going to be flying with her tonight when the sun went down. She looked around the yard.

All the others had shifted as well. Ace stood alone in the yard as his dragon and tears of gems flowed from his eyes. As he stood there crying, she knew just how he felt. After all this time, he was allowed to be just like his cousins and be a dragon as well. Tank too was alone in his shift. The two of them looked so alone that she wanted to go to them. And she might have if she weren't so afraid that she'd hurt someone in the process. She had to get used to her dragon before she would feel safe just moving around.

Stretching out on the lawn, she laid there while Cassian sat on her hand. She wasn't as large as she thought she'd be, but big enough that he looked dwarfed by her size. Having had enough of the dragon for now, she thought of her other self and changed back swiftly. She wasn't sure that she wanted to be just a human again, but she wanted to save up her strength for tonight when she learned to fly. Oh, how she was looking forward to that.

Lady Earth seemed to be pleased with what was

going on. Raven noticed that she went to each of them, telling them how proud she was of them and how she was looking forward to this evening to see them in the sky. Raven wished that they could go now, but knew that Cassian and the others were right; they'd scare the people of the town, and that wouldn't be a good thing when they were so close to getting the town back in shape as it should have been long ago.

She was also happy about the magic that would keep future mates from being in pain when they got the magic from the dragons. It hadn't bothered her, for she was the first of them to not have the pain, but she'd heard from the others and knew that it had been very painful for them, especially Kings and Skye, since they were supposed to be king and queen of their kind and had gotten a powerful amount of magic that put them down for four days. She'd hate to think how much pain that had been for her friends, and she was glad to be the first one who didn't have to experience that sort of agony.

Going back into the house when the other shifted back, she asked what would happen to the gems that the two cousins had cried. She'd always thought that it was a myth about dragon's tears, but was happy that it was true. She knew that the two of them were struggling, but wouldn't take any help from the family. She was happy that they were a part of the family now and couldn't be happier too that they fit right in with the rest of the group. Raven couldn't wait until they found their own mates so they could all be one big happy family.

"The court is set up for tomorrow to hear from Daniel. I'm to understand that he's going to represent himself at the trial." She asked if he thought that was smart. "I don't know if he has it in him to represent himself at work, much less at a trial that will determine his fate. I'm thinking that he's going to get the maximum amount of time for knocking you around, and then, on top of that, he'll have to be registered as a convict. I think that it's good that he'll lose his job over this. I can't imagine how he'd be treating his employees if he were to go back to work. I've not heard if he was going to have to take the classes again, but I would imagine that he'd have to do something while in prison."

"I'll just be glad that he's off the streets for a while. Maybe he'll learn something while there." She doubted it as soon as she said it. People like Daniel rarely learned anything that would benefit those around them. "Do you know how long he might get?"

"All I know is that the company that the two of you worked for said that he was to take the anger classes and pass them, or he'd be charged with assault. I guess since it happened on company property, they can take him to court over it. If he didn't pass the classes, then they would fire him and make sure that he got the maximum sentence for the crime that he caused."

"I heard from corporate yesterday. They said that they're sending me a check for compensation for the hospital stay, as well as a bonus for him being arrested before he hurt anyone else. I guess that's all right, but I'd rather they take care that they didn't hire people like him anymore." Cassian said that would be all right with him as well. "I guess we'll see."

Everyone was hungry again, and they had the faeries take care of their second dinner for them. They had thick subs with double meat that tasted so good after all the excitement of the evening. She was counting down the moments until it was dark enough to go out into the yard again and fly. It was something that she'd never done before, not even in a plane, but this was going to be the second-best thing that ever happened to her. The first had been meeting Cassian.

By evening, she was so worked up that she could barely contain her excitement. All the others had gone home so that they could learn to fly in their own back yards. They were going to meet up in the sky when it was time, and she was going to enjoy this even if she had to fly all on her own.

Not only did she have to learn to fly, but she had to learn how to use her wings, too. They were huge and would make things blow around if she used them too much. As she was learning how to walk on her two hind legs, she thought about all the things she was going to do once she was aloft. It took her over two hours before she was able to lift off the ground, and by then she was exhausted.

Disappointed in the way things were going, it was just as the sun was coming up that she was able to lift off enough to fly a few feet off the ground. By then, she was so tired that she didn't want to do any more of the lessons, but she was determined to get into the sky. Practicing in the backyard provided her with cover so that no one would see her, but it also made it so she had less room to get going so that she could be airborne. She was going to have to take this one day at a time, and she knew that someday she'd be able to fly with Cassian and have some fun. Flying was a great deal more work than she'd thought it would be.

Going to bed was all she could think about. Raven took a hot shower so that she'd not be as sore too and was asleep even before Cassian joined her in the bed. If she moved throughout the night, she didn't remember. Her body had shut down almost as soon as it got beneath the covers. She thought that she could sleep until noon the next day and not be as rested as she thought that she would need to be.

Chapter 6

Daniel was about as ready as he'd ever been for his day in court. He'd been encouraged by everyone that he'd been around to tell the judge his plan about having Raven working for him at the restaurant and how he was going to be taking her with him when he got promoted. There was no doubt in his mind that he'd be given a promotion because he'd be so calm about working that nothing would bother him. And if it did, he'd have Raven there to take up the slack, or his anger, as it were.

He had declined an attorney as he knew what he wanted to say while in the big room. Nothing was going to get in his way of making his point about how he was going to make things work for him. And it would. Just as soon as he could get Raven and her dumbass husband on board. There was no way he was going to believe that they didn't need the money as much as everyone did.

When the judge was brought into the room, he remained standing. Plenty was going on in the room, and he felt like he had the most to say and was glad that he was going to have this time in court. He had made him a list of points that he wanted to make, and when he made them, he was sure that the judge was going to see how much time and energy he'd put into this and waive the stupid classes that he had been made to take so that he could begin back at the restaurant where this all had begun. Blaming it squarely on Raven made him realize what a pain in the ass she'd been about the day of the great beating, and he was going to make sure she didn't get out of hand again. Some of his points were rules that she was going to have to follow in order for her to be his beating board.

One, and the most important, she was never to deny him his time in taking his anger out on her. She didn't have any say in where he was allowed to hit her, either. He would try his best not to mess up her face, but if he was having a particularly bad day, then she was going to have to deal with it. That's what she was there for in the first place, so she didn't have rules that he would follow. Not that he thought she was smart enough to make up any rules, but that was a different can of worms. The judge asked him what he wanted.

"I have a proposal that I'd like to talk to you about." He said that he didn't have time for his shenanigans today. "But this is for me not having to go to prison. I'd like to propose something to you so that I can get my job back and not have to take any more classes. It's a really good one, and if you do this for me, I'll tell everyone what a fine man you are, and they should vote for you."

"No one votes for me. I was appointed to this job. But it's men like you who give me a headache. Tell me what it is you want and I'll work from there. But you've already taken up more time than I had today, so don't expect me to go along with your plan even if it's the plan of the decade." He told him that he was going to love it as it would get two people back in the workplace and one more making money, so that he didn't have to borrow money for groceries. "I don't know what it is you're talking about, but do go on. We're all waiting on you with bated breath."

While he didn't have any idea what that meant, he was going to take it as a compliment. As soon as he picked up his notes on how to go on, he expounded on the bullet points as best he could. As he was explaining how things would go, he noticed that a lot of people were listening to him. They'd stopped what they were doing to notice him, and he felt empowered by it. The judge had even waved away his bailiff in favor of listening to him. That made him stronger in his conviction that this was going to work out in his favor. When he finished, he waited for the applause or something to let him know that everyone felt like this was something that would work for a lot of people. No more classes for anger management. Just find a person who needs money and have them work alongside you so that you'd have someone to take out your frustrations on. He was going to write a book about his idea and be a best seller. He could hear that famed —

"Are you telling me that you want to not have to spend any jail time for beating up a woman, nearly to death, I might add, because you think that having her with you to beat on when you're having a bad day is a good thing. Is that what you're saying?" He said that she'd be paid too by the company that he worked for, as she was useful for other things, like running a cash register. "Of course she is. And you say this woman is fine with this?"

"No, I think that's where you're going to have to step in and make her do it. I don't want to go to any more classes that are trying to teach me not to be angry again. I should be able to embrace my true self with her help, of course, and I'll be a much better employee for whoever I work for. I could use anyone, but she'd done such a good job at making me calmer before I figured that, why not just make her do it again? Besides, she thinks she can go to college and become an attorney, and she's just not smart enough for that."

"Is this woman here today?" He pointed to Raven. He also didn't know who she was, but for the big man who was with her. She'd changed so much that he thought she'd had work done on her face and body. "Mrs. Savage, is it?" She said that was her. "Can you come up here and tell me why you have agreed with something like this?"

"I didn't. He's been hounding me for weeks now, how I'm too poor to turn him down, and that I'm too stupid to make my own life outside of working for him as someone he can beat on." Daniel said that he'd have to make her work for him; it was the only way that his plan was going to work. "The day that he beat me, he actually calls it the day of the great beating. It was my last day at work, and I'd already clocked out for the day. He followed me all the way to my car to take out his anger and frustration on me. He wanted me to stay over and work so that he could take a two-hour lunch as he usually did. I had already made plans to get together with a couple of friends to celebrate my last day of work when he put me in the hospital."

"I've read the report on what happened to you that day. And now he's saying that he wants it to happen daily for you. Please tell me this isn't anything that you agreed to? I have to have more confidence in humankind than that." She said that she wasn't going to work for him as she had a full schedule she was going to work on. "Good for you. And good luck with becoming an attorney. Now let me deal with this young man."

"Your honor, see how she is? She thinks this is going to only benefit me when it will benefit a lot of people. She says she doesn't have to work, but I know better. She has worked in fast food for the past five years. You don't suddenly get rich working for a place like I work. There is no way she's going to make it as an attorney either. She's just too stupid." He said that she was smart enough to know better than to work for him. "She wouldn't be just working for me but for the entire company. If I'm a happy man, and beating her will make me happy, then the entire crew will be happy as well. And if I have a happy crew, then I have to have better sales than I would if I were screaming at them all the time. It will make sales better, which is the bottom line in places like where I would be working. That's another thing I'm going to need you to do: make sure that I have my job back with no more anger classes. I'm sure you'll see vast improvement in my demeanor when I'm working with Raven."

The judge looked like he was confused. He would gladly explain it to him again, but he asked him to be quiet for a few minutes. He'd gladly not say anything for hours if he got out of jail and got to work with Raven. He did wonder if anyone would work in her place, but decided that they had a history and that they were meant for each other. Daniel waited for the judge before he sat down. This was going to give him just what he needed in the world to be able to find a job and keep it. He did wonder if it would work for any job and thought about him writing a book again. He was sure that it would be a best seller in no time.

"I don't even know what to say to you, young man." He told him that he could explain it to him again if he was confused about what he wanted. "I got it. You want someone, this young woman here, to follow you around so that you can take your anger out on her and not other people. You also want me to make it so that you get your old job back, too, if I'm not mistaken."

"Yes. I loved that job, and I really think that I could do a good job in it with her around. She certainly did relax me the day of the great beating. I've never felt like I could fit in. I was so angry all the time. And well, when she told me no that she wasn't going to stay over and work for me, something in my head just exploded." He asked him what he'd done in jail in order to be so calm. "I've been keeping notes on those that have made me angry and how I was going to take it out on Raven when she starts working with me again. You noticed that I said working with me because it would be a partnership between the two of us."

"So you're saying that she can beat on you when she's angry or frustrated?" Daniel laughed. Because it was so funny to think that she would try to hit him. "I see. So this partnership would be all one-sided, where you get all the perks and she will spend a lot of time in the hospital."

"No, no hospital. I'll try not to hit her so hard that she ends up there, but she's going to have to be available twenty-four/seven. And her being in the hospital will not be something that I can take a chance on." He picked up his notes and saw that he'd written that down already. "No. She'll have to deal with any pain that I cause her or any hurts on her own. One day without her could cause a great many people to be harmed. We don't want that, do we?"

"No, I can see where that would cause you some issues." He seemed to be getting on board with the way things needed to be, and he asked him when they could get started on their wonderful life together. "Did you happen to ask her husband what he thinks about all this?"

"He's not for it. Claiming to be one of the Savages with all the money. Why would a person who has all the money in the world want to marry someone like Raven? She's pretty enough, but she's just too dumb to know what a good thing it is that I'm offering her and him. You'd have to show him the way it needs to be as well." The judge asked for Cassian Savage to stand up. He asked him what he thought of the idea. "I already told you that he's not in agreement with it. He seems to think that he and his wife are happy the way things are."

"If he so much as touches her with intent, I will kill him. He's done enough damage to her as it is, and I've had about enough of his ideas concerning Raven." Savage turned and looked at him. "I've told you this before. We're not going to be playing your little games. She's not going to be your playmate either. I find you to be sick in the head if you think that anyone is going to go along with you on this."

"The judge is all but convinced this is going to work." He said that he was not. He didn't think that it would work for anyone. "But you have to make it work for me. I just don't know how I'd keep from beating other employees if I have to work under those conditions."

"The company that you used to work for says that they will no longer employ you in any shape or form. Also, other places have contacted me to tell me that they don't want you in their restaurant as a guest, much less as someone who would work for them." He said that he was going to have to make them change their mind. He was going to be the best employee they had. "So long as you have someone that you can beat on, I guess."

"You make it sound like a bad thing. It's not, not really. The only person that will be getting hurt is Raven, and it's not like she's not going to be paid for her trouble." The judge said he wasn't going to entertain such a solution. "But you have to. If not, then I've wasted all this time. You don't want to have wasted your time on this, do you?"

"Just to hear you talking has made me realize that I'm getting too old for this stuff anymore. To think that you actually went to the trouble to write things down of what you wanted to say, as if it was a good thing." He said that he thought it was. "It's not. I don't know anyone who would think that this is a good idea and be able to live with it. Christ man, she's a human being. Did you ever consider that when you were coming up with this hairbrained idea?"

"She'd be getting paid. It's not like she wouldn't be compensated for her time." The judge just shook his head. "I don't think I've made myself clear on my points here. Let me go over them again so that you have an—"

"Oh, I have an idea of what's going on. You want to abuse this poor young woman because she told you no once, and you want to make her pay." Daniel said that wasn't all true. "I believe that I am telling the truth of the matter." He banged his gavel and told him to have a seat. "If you talk once more about this great idea that you've had, I'm going to put you in prison right now and hope they lose the key to your cell. Sit down and shut up."

Daniel sat, but he wasn't nearly finished with this. He knew what would make the company hire him back, and he'd gone to the trouble of writing it all down for the man. If he couldn't get on board with it, he was going to go over his head and make them listen to him and his plan.

~*~

"I can't believe that he sentenced him to ten years without the chance of parole. Then, he made him take anger management classes while he was in prison."

Raven sat on the couch in their living room, reeling from the verdict that had come down to Daniel. He'd been so angry that he'd demanded an hour in a cell with her so that he could be calmed again. She shivered every time she thought of what he would have been able to do to her in that hours' time. "Do you suppose that he'll find someone that he can beat on in jail?"

"Christ, I hope not. Can you imagine what that person would look like after a couple of days? Not to mention, I can't imagine that the people who run the prison would be too keen on that going on either. They'd have to do something like put him in solitary confinement to keep him from beating people all the time." Cassian laughed a little. "Or they might turn away from it happening, hoping that someone will take exception to what he's doing to another person. I don't know, but we have plenty of time for him to be gone. Then in the morning, we're going to go and see what Jason and the Connors get for their crimes."

Raven had heard all about the three people who had hurt Skye and Trevor. She also knew that much like Daniel, Jason Waggoner didn't think that he should be in prison because he'd killed a lot of people. He saw himself as a professional and didn't think that his being in prison was the way it should go for him. He also bragged about the people that he killed and that the Connors should have left it to professionals like him, so that they didn't get into trouble with the law. She thought that people were as strange as hell.

Tonight she was going to try again to have a lift off. It didn't bother her because the other women hadn't been able to do it either. She thought she knew what her problem was; she just didn't think of herself as a dragon, and she was having trouble thinking of herself as flying. She'd get there soon, she told herself, but it was just getting in the air that was keeping her down. Rolling her eyes at herself, she was going to do it tonight or know the reason why. She wanted to fly with Cassian.

For right now, she had three more chapters to read in her first class before they started on Monday. It wasn't as difficult to remember what she was reading as she thought it might be, so she was enjoying studying. Taking notes, too, on the chapters she'd been assigned to read was helping her, too. Also, in addition to the book that she had to read, there were three other books that she was going to have to take with her on the first day of classes. She was glad now that she'd downloaded the books on her computer so she'd not have as much to carry. She didn't think that all her classes were going to be this easy, but she was having fun getting ready for the hard stuff to come along.

"I have something for you." She asked Cassian what he'd gotten her, then told him that she didn't need anything. "I've been able to find you a complete set of law books for your office. The other cousins and

I went through our boxes of books and put together an entire set for you. Also, we've been able to find you some recent books, too, that you can use. All of us at one point or another have been some kind of attorney. Tank has the last attorney time under his belt, so he said that he remembers enough to help you with classes when you need it."

She went to her office to have a look around. There were hundreds of books that she could use, and she was excited to have them. She knew that they were expensive and hard to get all of them together, but they'd given her such a gift that she could hardly contain her happiness. Hugging Cassian, she told him how much she loved him for doing this for her.

"I love you, and it's my pleasure to do things for you like this. You're my life, and it makes me happy to see you so happy." She hugged him to her again and decided that she was in the perfect place to be held, and kept her arms around him. "You are my heart of all hearts, love, and I can't believe that you've found me when you did."

"I'm the lucky one. To think that I kept pushing you away all the time because I was afraid that you'd leave me. Now I can't stand a moment without you by my side, or I'll go insane." He said he felt the same way. "Good. Then we'll keep each other happy by staying close all the time. I just don't know what I'd do without you."

She played in the backyard with Cassian for several hours. By the time dinner was ready, she was covered in sweat and grass and felt like her legs were going to buckle. While she thought that things would get better soon, she was getting more frustrated every time she tried to fly, and all she did was tumble in the grass like she'd tripped over something. Then she heard that Kaida had gotten up in the air.

She reached out to her to find out how she'd done it. The men were doing a good job in teaching her, but she had a feeling that Kaida had figured something out on her own and would share it with her. As soon as she told her that she was ready to give up on it, then she could fly. Raven was so disappointed in herself that she wanted to sob. Going out into the yard, she decided that she wasn't going to listen to Cassian about it anymore and do things her own way.

It took her another frustrating two hours before she felt like she'd gotten it. Landing was still hard, but she knew if she could get up into the sky, the rest would be easy. After twilight, she decided that she'd waited long enough and had taken to the skies. It was the most freeing thing she'd ever done in her life, and she was never going to come back down to earth if it was the last thing that she did.

When Cassian joined her as his great dragon, they flew through the skies on their own until the others started joining them in pairs, one at a time. She was surprised to find that Skye's dragon was much larger than hers, but she found that she really didn't care. She was in the sky, where she felt she belonged.

Cassian and his cousins knew tricks that they could do that would have them soaring upward beyond the clouds and bring them down again at breathtaking speeds. She wasn't ready for that, but did play with them when they were at her level. The other women seemed to be doing well now that they'd figured out the flight thing, and she was happy that she had one more thing she could share with them as dragons.

They flew for hours, and she'd been able to land once without any trouble, but she was nervous about doing it again. Laying on the grass, she was glad for the darkness because there was no one to see how exhausted she was again. She knew that she'd get used to it, but for now, it was like she was exercising all the time, and it was wearing her out.

When Cassian joined her in the yard, she curled her dragon up close to his and closed her eyes. She told herself it would only be for a few minutes and that she only wanted to rest. The dreams started right away.

She was flying through the night sky when she came upon a group of farmers out in the fields. They were screaming at her about some kind of fire, but she was just too far away to hear them. Getting closer, landing on the ground next to them, they ran at her with pitchforks and hatches. Getting back into the sky seemed paramount, but she couldn't get her legs to work. Just as they were ready to stab her in the heart, she woke up from her dream and startled Cassian. She told him what she'd dreamt about.

"That doesn't happen all that much nowadays. As I said to you before, they know that we're dragons, but I don't think they really care." She asked about the way they were set to kill her. "I think you've had a great deal of drama happening in the last few months, and everything seems like someone is out to kill you. It's a small wonder that you don't have dreams about being beaten up more often, what with all the things that Daniel has been saying about you and how you were going to help him."

"That is true. He did tell me every time I saw him how much he'd enjoyed beating the shit out of me when I'd quit." She thought of that day and shivered. "I wonder what makes a person think like that. I mean, to think it's justified in treating someone else like they mean nothing to them."

"You would have meant a great deal to him. I'm not saying that he was right in thinking that you'd calm him down, but I do wonder what would have happened to you had you not been enough for that one time he really lost his temper. I believe that he would have eventually killed you. Then the only reason that he would have been sorry was because you were gone, and he had no one else to beat on for a while. But I'm sure he would have found just that perfect person again until he got so angry again that he killed the next person as well. It would have gone on for years had he been able to get anyone to go along with his plans."

"I'd never seen his temper until that time. He'd had one and would rant and rave about things not going his way. It was why we were all happy when he left us for a couple of hours. So much got done, and when he returned, he was always in a better mood. However, I don't want to think about what he was doing in his time off from work. I hope it wasn't that he was beating someone like the homeless to make himself feel better." She looked around the yard and was shocked to see that at some point she'd shifted back to her human form.

"The magic does that for you in the event that you're found while resting. Someone would come across your big beast and kill you while you were out. The magic puts you back to human form so that you can rest easily and not have to be on guard as much while as a dragon. Dragons of old used to fall into a large area of cattle and then change into their other form to rest. No one would think that a human person would destroy so many cattle as it would take to fill a full-sized dragon." She laughed about that, thinking that it was funny that dragons were so smart. He laughed with her, telling her another story about dragons. "There are water dragons that used to come upon great ships that would be carrying loads of fish. They'd of course destroy the ship to get to the fish and whatever else they had going on. Then, when they were found, usually up on the shore of some tropical island, they'd live there for a while, knowing that food was only a dive away."

"I'd love to hear stories like that. From when you were younger." He said that the four of them, his brother and cousins, would have adventures all the time. "I bet you did. You should write them down and sell them as fantasy. I know that I'd read them all."

They talked about his adventures as a younger dragon until the others left. They had things to do this morning at the courthouse, and so did Cassian and she. They had made arrangements to be married by the judge who was presiding over the Connor and Waggoner trials today, and wanted their part just out of the way. The only people who knew what they were doing were Brenin and Tucker, and Kaida. They were going to serve as witnesses. Raven felt like her life was starting over on a good note, and she couldn't have been happier.

Chapter 7

Jason sat stunned on his cot. He knew that he was going back to prison someday, not that he wanted it to happen, but to have ninety-eight life sentences was more than he thought anyone should get. Then he added on without parole. Ninety-eight lifetimes, he was going to be living in a prison cell. That was more lives than he had. He looked up at someone when they said his name. He couldn't focus on who it was until they told him.

"It's Skye Savage. You asked to see me." Had he? He didn't know why he'd do that since she was the one who had gotten him caught. Thinking hard, he tried to remember what he'd wanted to see her about. "If you don't want to talk to me, then I'm going home. I have to admit, I'm thrilled with the verdict and how much time you're getting." Then he remembered why he'd wanted to see her.

"You wouldn't die. And I know several times when you were in my sights, but I just couldn't get you to die. You should have been dead long ago." She said that she was just lucky. "No, it's more than that. You don't understand. I shot you several times, and you never would just die like you should have. I'm betting now you had someone watching over you, and that's why when I killed you, you never stayed dead."

"Then I don't understand what it is you're telling me. What do you mean you shot me several times? You just missed, that's all." He shook his head and told her that he never missed her. She'd been shot. "Well, obviously, you did miss because here I stand."

"No one is that lucky. You had to have some magical shit going on, and that's what saved you. I'm betting right now if I were to shoot you, you'd just walk away. There wouldn't be any way I'd miss with you standing this close." She took a step back. "I don't have a gun, you idiot. How would that even happen? I'm in a jail cell, just like the one I'm going to be spending the rest of my life in, thanks wholly to you."

"How is you killing all those people, my fault? You were killing people before I ran away with Trevor. I suppose next you're going to tell me you killed him as well." He said he never would have killed Trevor, as he was the money maker. She was just collateral damage. "You're mistaken, that's all. You couldn't have killed me now anyway. I'm immortal."

"You've always been immortal." She looked like she'd thought of something, and he knew when whatever she was thinking occurred to you. "What? What did you just remember? I have a right to know since this is all your fault."

"I don't know how you think this is my fault, but you might be right in me being immortal all along." He asked her what she meant. Instead of answering him, she called out for someone called Lady Earth or something like that. Suddenly, there was a woman standing next to Skye. She explained to her what he'd said to her.

The woman looked like magic. Not magical so much as she was magic. There was a light surrounding her that made you think she was just good. Not good at something, but good to people, creatures of the earth, and anything else that roamed around. When she frowned at Skye, even the creases in her forehead looked beautiful. Because in that moment, he realized that she was the most beautiful creature of any kind he'd ever seen. She turned to look at him.

"You never were a good person, where you, Jason Waggoner." His name, one that he'd been proud of since he'd learned to kill people, sounded like a curse. "I remember you pulling the wings off my faeries and little brownies. No, you were never a good person at all."

"You saved her." She said that one of her faeries had saved her. "I knew it. I was better than that all along."

"That's no reason to be bragging about. You were a terrible man. Burying your dead in my lands. The land there is forever contaminated because of what you did to it." He laughed, feeling better about things all the way around. "What do you think will happen to you when you go to prison? I shall have a faerie watching over you so that you can't die until you're a very old man. What do you think of that?"

"I killed her, and you saved her. I knew I was better than that." Then it occurred to him what she'd said to him. "No. You can't do that to me. I have the right to die when my time comes. And I plan on making it as short as time possible."

She snapped her fingers, and a small yellow faerie appeared. He could always see them. Since he was just a little boy. Jason would catch them and do just what she said, pull their wings off of them, then kill them by smashing them with a big rock.

"This is Snow. She'll be watching over you for the next phase of your life. You'll be the oldest living inmate at the prison. Won't that be wonderful for you? You'll live out one hundred and four years with her watching over you." He screamed no, that would be more than his life was now. "So it will. And it will not be enough to cover all the lives that you took when you were free."

He was thinking of spending the next sixty-plus years in prison and wanted to die right then. There was no way that they'd make him sit in a prison cell for that long. He was going to have to do something that would set him free from the place. Suicide by cop was the only thing that he could think of.

"It won't work. Nothing you think of will get you killed before I say you may die." He asked her why she was doing that to him. "Because of the way you treated one of mine. Skye has been my child since the day she was born, and I will continue to watch over her for the rest of her life. Think of this. The people who sentenced you will long be gone before you are taken out in a body bag. I don't usually take retribution out on humans, but you've caused me enough pain and sorrow to last more lifetimes than you originally got from the man in the long cape. And you will live. I have decreed it."

"I'll still be alive when Skye is dead. That makes me feel better." He laughed and smiled at the otherworldly creature. "All your retribution is for naught since I'll still outlive her."

"Nay, you will not. She'll be around like my other dragons for longer than that. Forever and a day, she will still be here. While you are nothing more than dust, she will be free to live her life as she sees fit. Using her magic, as I have hope that she will, so that there are more dragons born to fill the skies of my realm, where they can be as free as they wish." He laughed again, feeling like insanity was getting the better of him. Dragons? She couldn't outlive him. How could that be fair, he asked. "It is fair. As I said, you have killed people, humans, and shifters alike and buried them in my earth. Then you tried to kill my darling Skye. I've had great plans for her since her birth."

"You can't be serious? This isn't right. There are no such things as dragons." Suddenly, he found himself outside of his cell with her hand on his forehead. There in front of him was a dragon. One as scary and beautiful as he'd ever seen in any book. When it turned and looked at him, it opened its mouth wide. Fire flew from his mouth and toward him. His screams woke him up, and he ended up back on his cot all alone. "There is no way that I just got burnt by a dragon."

But he could feel his skin burning like he'd been in the sun too long. Looking down at him, he wasn't the least bit surprised to find blisters along his arms and hand. Lying down on the cot, covering himself up from any more visitors, he rolled with his back to the door and closed his eyes. Something was wrong with him, or he was really seeing dragons. And beautiful women who said he was going to live for a very long time.

When he woke, he was still hot. Throwing off the covers, he saw Snow up by the ceiling of his cell. He thought about trying to kill it, but she'd just send another. He fully believed that the woman had been correct in her telling him that he was going to live too long behind bars. There was no way that could be legal, and yet he believed that it was going to happen.

Oh, his life had taken a terrible turn.

When his meals were brought to him, he ignored them. He'd been told when he tried starving himself before that they'd not allow it. Then Snow told him that she had magic that would force him to eat his meals. They wanted him to be healthy when he made his way to prison. Which, if he remembered correctly, would be tomorrow. He sat up to eat his meal and decided that there wasn't enough magic in the world to make him eat whatever had turned up as his meal.

"You'll eat it." He found himself eating the meal, and while not enjoying it, wanted seconds. As he laid down again, his mind just too worn out to think much more, Snow began talking to him. "Did you remember that the Connors got two life sentences? They'll not last long in prison as they are already old in human years." He didn't care and said as much.

"Why do they get to live out a good short life, and I have to live for what seems like forever?" He was told that they couldn't allow him to live forever, as that wouldn't be something that humans did. "So it was on the table that I lived forever? Your boss is very vindictive, don't you think? I never killed Skye, much to my heartache. But she's treating me like I've done it several times over."

"But you did. Kill her, I mean. The only reason that she is alive now is because of the faeries that were with her each time you tired. You were not all that good at some of the times you took her out. It was easy for us to make sure that she lived for a great many days more when you were out of the way." It figures. She'd have someone treating her to magic while he kept trying to make her dead. "Not that it matters now, however. She is immortal and has enough magic that she could kill you, no matter if she was with you or not. She's powerful in her own right."

"Figures. Everyone has powers but me." Snow told him that was the way it was to be. "How much magic do you have? I'm betting not much for how small you are. You probably can't do much at all for all your professed power." She laughed at him.

"I know what you're doing. I've been around humans all my life and know when someone is trying to bait me. It won't work. I'm much smarter than you are and can beat you at your own game. I will not kill you because I like the plan that is in place to keep you living for a long time." He said it wasn't fair. "I believe it to be very fair. What you did to some of your victims was very wrong. And three times you simply killed because you were bored. That is not the work of a good man."

"I'm not a good man." Snow neither agreed nor disagreed with him. Instead, she sat on the windowsill and left him to himself. Putting the now-empty tray on the floor and sliding it out of his room, he laid back again, this time with his hands behind his head. "I've done things that no human would ever do without the money that came along with it. I was paid well for what I could do better than anyone I knew."

He thought of all the people that he killed and thought that it was going to be worth it to be able to say he'd murdered so many before his thirtieth birthday. However, he was going to pay for it now; living out a long life behind bars would take so much from him. He needed the freedom to roam and wasn't going to get that while in prison. He wondered briefly if he'd be in a wheelchair when he was as old as dirt.

"Nay, you will be as spry as you are now." He didn't like the little creature reading his mind, and she told him that it was just too easy. "I will keep you company for your long years, too. We'll talk about many things that will be going on. And I will keep you updated on Skye and her family as well. It's the least I can do after you failed so many times."

"I didn't fail. I killed her several times, you said." She told him that, yet she still lives. "She lives by magic and nothing more."

"As you will live and die by magic and nothing more." You'll live these years that the queen has given you without fear of dying. That should make you feel better. You'll have pain, but not as much as dying would give you." He looked up to where she was sitting and wanted to scream at her. But he knew that the cells were being monitored. What would it look like if he were suddenly screaming at the top of his lungs? He had a sudden thought. "It won't work for you. You cannot make them want to kill you, no matter how insane you try to make yourself be."

"Go to hell." He decided that he wasn't going to talk to the little creatures anymore. He knew that at some point he was going to, but for now, he was happy with his decision. The thing was going to annoy him enough that they would think him addled in his old age. "Christ. That's going to be a very long time from now."

~*~

"I'm satisfied with the way things went today." Raven was curled up next to Cassian in the bed. It was just after midnight, and they were both tired. "I know that Lady Earth said that he'd live a long time, and that's good too. He should be made to suffer as much as he possibly can. Skye is certainly going to be sleeping a good deal better with him gone from her life."

"She'd been having nightmares since she and Kings got together. Some nights she will lash out at him just so she can make herself feel safe in her dreams." She told Cassian that she'd never had a nightmare that bad. "I've had them before of my parents. The only way that I could get rid of them was to sleep with my brother nearby. Brenin brought me out of the dreams before they got to be too bad."

"He's a wonderful man and my good friend."

Cassian kissed her on her shoulder and moved his mouth to her throat. She loved it when he would lick her there. It made her shiver in anticipation of what he might do next. "You're suddenly not too tired, are you? I mean, I thought you said you were exhausted."

"I am, but not for you." He slid over her, and she turned on her back to look up at him. "I want to make love to you tonight. Make the day end on a special note that you and I can share."

"I love you, Cassian." He said that he loved her as well. "You're my life, I hope you know that."

"I do. And you are my breath. I couldn't survive without you by my side." She bared her throat to him when he was kissing her other shoulder. "You taste like a dream, and I'm going to make sure that I don't miss a part of you tonight."

As he made his way down to her breasts, she felt her nipples harden painfully. When he suckled them into his mouth, rolling the hard tips with his tongue until she cried out with it. She loved it when he did that to her. Making his way down her body, Raven spread her legs for his weight. He moved more down her body until he was between her legs and at her pussy. She felt it weep with the knowledge of what he was going to do to her now.

When he licked her from gate to clit, she cried out again. The small, hard punch to her system was just the release she needed to go on. As he suckled her clit into his mouth, his fingers entered her, and she moaned. This is what she'd been wanting all day. Her man to eat her and fuck her at the same time.

Raven came so many times that she lost count. One moment, she'd had enough, and the next she'd be crying out with another earth-shattering release. It was too much and not enough at the same time. Bowing up off the bed, she grabbed Cassian by the hair and pulled his head up to her mouth. Kissing him, tasting herself on him, gave her another release like none other.

"Take me." He said that he would and moved between her legs again. Wrapping her legs around his hips and locking her ankles around him, she sat up when he did. Sitting on him like she was, his cock was between them and hard as stone. Reaching down to fist him, he cried out when he came enough for her to use his cum to continue to slide up and down his cock. "I want you to come all over me, then fuck me."

"Yes." The one-word answer was hissed at her, and she couldn't believe how heady she was feeling. When he slid her up enough that he could fill her, she cried out as he slowly filled her. She would swear under oath if asked that he was larger than he'd ever been before, and she wanted him to take her. "Fuck me, Raven. Fuck me until we both come, then I'm going to pound you until you hurt."

She moved her hips in time to his rising up off the bed. It was slower than she wanted, but it was so much more than anything she'd had. As she fucked him, rolling her hips back and forth, he pressed her breasts together and suckled at them one at a time until they were painful. Running her hand through his hair, she held him close to her as he rolled them to her back.

With her hips still around his, he took her slowly. She wanted to be pounded as he had promised, but this was wonderful too. As he kissed her mouth and did things to her throat that she'd only dreamed of, Raven begged him for a release. She needed to be able to do that so that she could breathe again.

When he pulled her arms above her head and locked them in one of his hands, she held onto the headboard while he made love to the rest of her body. He touched her breasts and her ribs. Tickled her thigh with his fingers and suckled at her earlobe as well. There was no part of her body that he missed. And while doing so, she was as tense and overwhelmed by him as she'd ever been in all the times they'd made love.

"Tell me what you want." She told him that she needed to come. "Will you come with me? Let me feel your pussy milking my cock when you do?"

"Yes, anything you want." He moved deeper inside of her, and she could swear that he was at the back of her throat. "Please, Cassian. I need to come hard, and I want you to come with me."

He fucked her slowly, building up his tempo as

he went. By the time she put her hands on his shoulders to hold on to him, he was taking her hard enough that the bed moved. Digging her nails into his back, trying her best to hang onto him. She screamed out a release that made the room around her spin and the darkness swallow her up.

She was out only for a few seconds. Waking, she knew that the climax that she'd had wasn't going to be the best one. It was coming, and as soon as she reached out for it, Cassian told her that he was coming with her. Everything in her body stopped moving.

Colors bounced behind her eyelids. Stars sprinkled down over the two of them like they were skyborn. Even as she was coming down, her body limp with release, she came again and again so quickly that she didn't have time to breathe or have her heart beat. If this was the way that she was going to die, she was happy for it.

Waking with Cassian atop her, she moved until he did. All he did was roll over onto his back, taking her with him. If asked, she would have said that her body was dead and her mind hadn't caught up with it as yet. But she was so relaxed that she didn't have the strength to lift her hand up to brush the hair off her face. Everything was just too loose.

"It's a good thing that we're immortal. I think that would have done us in if not for that." She giggled; she couldn't help it. He looked at her with one eye open. "You're very cruel, I hope you know that."

"Why?" He told her. "I doubt very much that would be considered cruel to be too beautiful to resist. That would be like me saying that you're too sexy for people to resist. I hope they do for your sake, but you are just too sexy."

"Thank you." She cried out when he swatted her on her ass. "That was for nearly killing me. I think, however, that I'm broken in some places."

"I am as well." She moved enough to know that she didn't have the strength that she hoped she had to make it to the bathroom. "I'm going to have to lay here for the next ten years or so just so that I can heal."

They did talk a bit more about how they'd broken one another. Joking about how sex had done them in and they'd never be able to have it again. When Cassian said that he really needed to get up, she begrudgingly moved off him in favor of getting to the bathroom before him. As soon as she stood up, however, she regretted not doing as she had suggested before and laid there for the next decade. She was as weak as a kitten.

The two of them finally made it to the bathroom about half an hour later. The bottom of her feet were sore, and her arms were weak from holding him so tightly. Getting back into the bed, she was happy that some of the magic that the faeries had put in the room was to make the bed, as soon as they were both out of it came into play. They had messed up the bed enough that she didn't know which way was up. Cassian joined her some minutes later, after complaining about how sore he was, too.

Cassian held her while he slept. She was too awake now to sleep, so she was able to get out of bed without hurting herself the second time. Going downstairs after dressing, she was going into her office when something occurred to her. She was starving.

Glad for the faeries that seemed to be up all the time, she was given a sandwich and a glass of milk to eat and drink. As soon as she finished that, she got herself an apple to munch on while she made her way to the office. She had something that she wanted to do, and it wasn't going to take her much time to do it. Opening her laptop, she opened the program that got her into her classes online. Clicking on the one that she'd been working on earlier today, she was finally able to answer the questions that had been plaguing her all afternoon. She just needed to get out of her mind for a while.

Raven was still at her computer when Cassian joined her in her office. Smiling up at him, he asked her what was wrong. Telling him what she'd been able to do, he nodded and told her that he was starving. Going to the kitchen with him, she sat and watched him eat. They had both worked up quite the appetite.

"Tomorrow...I guess today I have to meet Ace

at one of the buildings that we purchased recently. He thinks that there is someone living in it." She asked him how many there were. "Two that he thinks have been living there for about three months. I didn't see anything when I was there, but I was looking for structural damage rather than someone living there. It won't take much to get them out, but it's hard on him thinking that they have nowhere else to go."

"Maybe we can get them into the shelter." He said that they were filled up this time of year, what with school being out of session. "Why would school have anything to do with it?"

"Because with fees and books, some people just can't afford things like rent and electricity. I've seen it before. It's a terrible shame that we don't have it where there were no fees for kids to go to school, but that's the way things are. I don't know that that's the issue with these people, but it's something that I've run into before." She said that broke her heart. "Mine too. I hate to see anyone homeless, but families hurt me more. Kids don't understand, and there is little to nothing that can be done about it once they're out on the streets. There should be help for them when they're thinking of leaving. Usually, once they leave the house, the landlord won't take them back, no matter what happens."

"I should go out and find him to tell him that I'm not happy." He kissed her on the nose, and she smiled at him. "Is there really nothing we can do for them? For all we know, it could be a woman and her child that is out of housing."

"It could be a man and his child, too, but I understand what you mean. It would be nice if we could help everyone, but some people just don't want to be helped. They think they have a handle on things, and they don't see that their family is suffering." She asked him if he knew who was in the building. "No, I don't. I wish I did. I'd have a place for them if I could figure it out. But we'll have to go there today and run them off. We're hoping to not have to involve the police too. They can make matters worse sometimes."

"I would imagine. They have rules to follow, and you guys just want them gone." He said that was it in a nutshell. "I feel bad for them. It would be terrible to have to live on the streets. I've never had to do that, but I know people that had. Skye and Trevor did for a long time, didn't they?"

"Yes. There are others, too, that have made it work, too." She sat in his lap while he held her and told her how much he loved her. "I'm exhausted again. How about we head up to bed and try our best to get some sleep? It's been a long day, and I'm happy to have a bed that I can sleep in."

"As am I. We're blessed with a wonderful life, you and I." He said that he'd carry her up to bed, but he didn't think that he could make it. "I can walk. I want to hold you while we go up so that I don't miss a second of telling you how much I love you."

When she got back in bed, the covers were made up once again, she held Cassian to her until she was ready to sleep again. Tomorrow was going to be a long day if she didn't get any sleep, and she willed herself to relax. Smiling to herself, she wondered how she'd gotten so tense again when she'd had the best sex of her life. Rolling to her back, she counted dragons until she was dozing off. Tomorrow was going to be a great day, she told herself, and was happy that she had a roof over her head tonight.

Chapter 8

Brenin watched his brother talk to the woman and man. They didn't want to move on, and the mister told them that he didn't want to work either. A job was offered to them both, and they both declined, saying that it was nicer to have free rent than to have to work out something with a job. It didn't make sense to him either, but he watched the two of them in the event that things got out of hand. And he had a feeling that it would, too, for some reason.

"Call the police. We've done all we can do for them." Nodding, he pulled out his cell phone to call when the man pulled out a gun. Unsure what he was going to do with it, he put the phone to his ear and told them what he wanted. The police said that they'd be there in less than three minutes, and Brenin hoped they would be. Things went from bad to worse when he held Ace to his chest with the gun pointed at his head. "You don't want to do that."

"Yes, I do." Cassian was trying to reason with the older man, but he wasn't having it. "I told you we were just fine here and for you to move on. Then you called the police like we don't have any rights."

"You don't actually. You're squatting in a building that is up for demolition. It's being demoed for a reason. The walls are structurally unsound." Even before talking to the people, Cassian had determined that it wasn't worth trying to renovate, as the load-bearing walls had been shaken and couldn't hold up their own weight. "Just put the gun down, and we'll give you three days to vacate the building. Otherwise, the police are going to arrest you for trespassing."

"We weren't trespassing. This place is ours. We been living here for six months." That didn't sound right, but Brenin didn't say anything. He was watching the woman dance around the man with the gun. He was fearful that she might well get shot the way that her man, that's what she kept calling him, kept waving it around while holding onto Ace. "You guys just move on, and we'll pretend like this didn't happen. This here is our building, and we're going to live in it until we say otherwise."

"That's not going to work." Cassian looked over at him before addressing the man again. "I'm going to shift and take you out if you don't let my cousin go. He's a good man, and he'll be as pissed off as I am if you happen to shoot him. Now let him go so that the police can take you away."

"I ain't afraid of no shifter. My wife is a shifter too. You just try and hurt me, and she'll take you out. She's a big wolf." No, she wasn't, Brenin could smell that she was just as human as the man was. "You try anything and I'm going to give her the command to kill you, then it'll be all over. This man here in my arms will be dead, and so will the two of you."

"You must think she's pretty fast if you think she's going to get by me and my brother. And she's not a wolf. Neither of you are shifters." He asked him how he knew that, and Cassian said that he could smell them. "But then you both stink, so I could be wrong about that. But you're not going to be able to touch us, and Ace will not die. You remember that, don't you, Ace? That you can't die?"

He wondered what Cassian was going on about when he had a look at the other man. Ace was showing signs of fear, and it looked like he'd forgotten that he was indeed immortal. He might well have, too, if he had a gun pointed at his head the way that Ace was. He tried moving closer to the two of them and was stopped when the police pulled in. He didn't think this was going to end well for the couple.

"Mister, put that gun down on the ground and let Mr. Savage go." One of the officers from the first car was doing all the talking now. He wondered if he remembered that Ace wasn't going to die when he spoke again. "Put the gun down, or we're going to shoot you dead. Do you hear me? We will no matter if you let the mayor go or not. You'll be a dead man."

"Shoot me in the chest." Brenin started to tell

them not to do what Ace was saying when he realized that it was the most brilliant idea he could come up with. "Just don't shoot me in the head, that'll hurt, but you can shoot me in the chest and I'll be just fine."

"We're not going to shoot you in the head or chest." The police officer turned and looked at him. "He's been hurt, hasn't he? He's been hurt by that man, and now he wants us to shoot him. We can't do that."

"I can." The officer, he thought that his name was James, said that he wasn't going to shoot anyone either. "But he won't die. You know what we all are. I promise you, if you shoot him in the chest, nothing... how about you shoot him in the leg? He'll limp around for a little while, but not all that long. Just shoot Ace in the leg, and that will bring the man behind him down."

"Are you insane? I'd lose my job if I were to shoot the mayor. We all like him, too. He's gotten us money enough that we can have new vests. This one here that I'm wearing. No, I'm not going to shoot him anywhere. We'll just have to think of something else." He asked him if Cassian or him could shift. "Into a dragon? No siree Bob. No one is going to be shifting into a big assed dragon either. You just get that thought out of your head right now. A dragon would cause some damage."

"We were going to take the building down anyway. You'd be saving us money." He was trying to distract the officer and the man so that Cassian could get closer to him and take the gun. James said he wasn't going to have it. "The mayor would be happy too that both the building is down and the man is no longer holding a gun to his head. I'm betting that he'll—"

"What the hell are you yammering on about? There ain't no body going to shift because I'll kill this man if you do. Is that what you want? Me to kill this here man?" James told him that he didn't want anyone shot. "Why don't you get back in your car and drive away. I'll think about releasing this here man, if you were to let us live in the building until we want to quit it. That way, nobody gets shot."

"I don't think it's going to work out that way. You've got the mayor in your arms, and we like this one. He's been getting things done." James looked at Cassian, then back at the man. His wife was dancing around, screaming at the top of her lungs about how everyone was going to be shot. "Can you please tell your missus to quiet down? She's giving me a powerful headache, and I'd hate to have her get hurt."

"Did you just threaten to hurt my wife? That's not right. And she likes to scream. It's part of who she is." Cassian was nearly to the man when the woman suddenly jumped on Cassian's back and screaming again. Brenin did the only thing that he could do when the man pointed the gun at his brother and shifted. It was over almost as soon as he touched the ground as his dragon.

"I don't know how to even fill out a report on this." James was nervous, and Brenin was trying his best not to laugh. He figured that if he did, the man would shoot him; he seemed to be that touchy. "Can you shift back to a real person, Brenin? I'd feel so much better if you did."

He went from beast to man in a few heartbeats. Nodding at him when he was done, James held out a clipboard that was trembling in his hand. He was still going on about the paperwork that had to be filled out while his partner arrested the man and the woman who had caused this all.

"Nobody is going to believe me when I tell them that I saw one of the Savage dragons and that he knocked a big building over with his tail." He told him he was sorry about that, but he didn't have much control over his tail at times. James glared at him. "Am I supposed to be happy that things ended without anyone being shot? I don't think so. I saw a big dragon scare a man nearly to pissing himself. Myself included in that, and I have to write up a report on what happened."

"Just say that we helped you as best we could." Again, the glare and Brenin laughed. "I'm sorry, James, but if you could have seen the look on your face when I shifted, then you'd be laughing too."

"I don't think this is the least bit funny, Brenin. What if you had hurt someone? You'd not be laughing then, would you?" He said that no one was hurt at all. And no shots were fired. "You're not helping me. Someone is going to ask questions, and I don't know what to tell them. Do I mention the dragon or not? What if someone asked me to describe you? I wouldn't even know where to begin. Big is all I'd be able to tell them. And you had big teeth."

"You'll be fine, James. I promise you no one will care now that an unsafe building is down and the mayor is safe. He is, too. Nothing happened to him at all." Another glare and another burst of laughter from him. "I don't know what you're so upset about. I told you that I was a dragon and that I was going to shift."

"I didn't believe it." He asked him what he meant. "I know that we all know that you're something other than human, but I don't think that any of us believed that you were dragons. Oh, it was in my mind that you were dragons, but I just didn't believe it until I saw him. You're a big fucking dragon, Brenin."

"Yes, I am. And you should know that I'd never harm you ever because you're a good man." He did chuckle a little when he thought of the man trying to get away from his dragon. He actually tossed the gun at him like that was going to be something that would have stopped him from coming after him. "What do you need me to do? You know that I'd do anything you need so that you're not going to be in trouble. I don't believe that the mayor will say anything to you about paperwork if you don't do it."

He looked at him, and he could see that James was on the verge of tears. He wasn't helping him right then while he was trying to distract him from what had happened. He was as sorry for that as he'd been about trying to save his brother from being hurt by shifting. His brother was his world, and he'd die before he let anything happen to him. Brenin told James that.

"I know that you would." He seemed calmer then, like he'd resigned himself to believing there were dragons in his town. "You really are a dragon. And the rest of you are, too, aren't you?"

"Yes, we are." He waited to see if he was going to say anything else, and when he didn't, he spoke to him again. "We're good men, too, that just happen to be able to shift into great dragons. Nothing more than that."

"Sure, that's such a little thing, you being able to shift into...I just can't wrap my head around seeing a dragon. I don't want to see it again, mind you, but if more bad guys knew what you were, we'd have nothing so much as a jaywalker in our town. We'd have only to take you to show and tell at the high school, and you'd bet that they'd take care to be on the right side of the law." He shook his head. "I'm losing it again. I need to have a seat."

He sat down on the hood of his cruiser and looked around toward the building that had come down when he'd landed near it. The couple had been lucky that there hadn't been a good storm come through, or they might well have been crushed. Cassian had been right in saying that it wasn't in good shape.

He'd told James that it was his tail that brought it down, but it was the shaking of the ground beside it. Yes, they were all lucky it didn't come down on some unsuspecting person while they were inside the thing. Or even on Ace and Cassian when they'd been inspecting the building. They couldn't die, but they would have been hurt badly had they been inside when it came down.

Hugging his brother when he was close enough to do so, he told him he loved him as well. He didn't do that nearly enough, tell people that he cared for them, and was going to make it a point to do so when he had the opportunity. You never knew what the next day was going to bring to you, and he was going to make sure that those around him knew that he thought well of them.

~*~

Cassian knew that Raven was going to be upset with him. He'd not gotten hurt, but he nearly had been shot. Not even telling her that he couldn't die would make her happy with him about trying to get a gun from a disturbed man and his wife.

"You want me to tell her?" Brenin was still laughing off and on, and he couldn't help but laugh with him. James had been really freaked out, and he was still going on about how he'd seen a dragon. "I don't think she'll be any less upset with you for doing what you did, but I can tell her for you."

"Nah, I got it. I'm just trying to work in when I tell her that I can't die. I think she's going to be thinking with her human brain instead of her dragon one and remember about that part." Brenin nodded and said that he was glad he was all right. "I am too. Thanks for saving me. It was funny when I think about the look on James' face when you shifted." The two of them laughed again.

"They arrested those two people. I don't suppose you noticed that the woman was totally naked, did you? That scared me more than anything when I did shift. I wondered if she thought that she was going to sacrifice to me or not." The two of them were in a mood, and if they kept it up, they were going to be in trouble with all the women of the family. Joking about everything wasn't a good thing. "I guess the police have had trouble with them before, setting up their homes in places that have been abandoned. I asked about the shelter house, and he said that they won't take them because they cause too much trouble. I can see that too. She's very loud."

They had to fill out a report on what happened, but were to leave the part about the dragon out. It had taken them both over an hour to get it right, and even then, James was a little worried about what the higher-ups would say when they read it. He didn't see what the problem was. They'd got them out of the building, he thought with a chuckle.

He and his brother had been dropped off at the stationhouse when they were finished. Then, after the report was given to James, they decided to have some lunch. He was surprised that he'd not heard from Raven in all that time, but he knew that she was spending the day with the other wives in getting things squared away for the Fall Fair that they were working on for late September. He might well be lucky, and she'd not heard yet. However, he wasn't counting on that.

He loved hanging out with his brother. It had been a while since he'd had the time to be just the two of them, and he was liking it. Brenin was younger than him by a few days, but they never talked about Cassian being the older of the two. It just didn't matter to them. Brenin asked him about finding a mate.

"Are you looking? I would have thought that you'd seen every female in this town at one point or another." He said that he was sure that he had, but was looking around outside of their circle. "Good idea. I didn't know that you were actively looking for someone to be with."

"I'm lonely. Not just that, but I'm bored with my life. I have a house that I like, friends and family that I adore, but something is missing from my personal life that I can't seem to fill. Like a void that I have." He said that he was sorry. "I don't mean to make you feel bad. It's just the way things are. I might be next or last; I have no idea, but it's great living through you guys with your mates. I'm betting she's out there, hoping anyway, but when is she coming to me that I find frustrating."

"I'm glad to see that you've not given up on finding her. I was at that point in my life, I think. Where I just didn't care if I got up in the morning and cleaned myself up. I just, well, I was just bored like you said. But I did have hope because the others had found their other half." He said that's what keeps him going. "It did me. Knowing that someday, hopefully, I'd find her or she'd find me, and I'd be as happy as Tucker and Kings. They are happy, don't you think?"

"I do. But I have to admit, you and Raven have a stranger relationship than the other two. You don't seem to have to be in each other's business like the other two. I see Tucker and Kaida together all the time. And Kings is with Skye twenty-four seven. Like they can't breathe without each other around all the time."

"I never noticed that about them. But now that you mention it, I see it. But Raven and I like to be together. I think it's because she wants to be independent from me. She's said that the entire time that I was trying to make her believe in me. That she didn't want me to hold her back on the things that she wanted to do. When she starts her classes in a couple of days, I'm going to be seeing less of her, and I'm all right with that, too. Because the time that we do spend together is better because of it. Understand?" He said that he did and looked around the area that they were sitting in before speaking again.

"I'm going to invest in a couple of things that Trevor told me about. I'm not in need of the money, but I'd like to know that it's there when I need it." He said that he did understand that. "Forever seems like a short amount of time sometimes. Like all the years that we were waiting for something to happen. Avoiding our parents. It's been a long time in coming, this life that I'm looking forward to. I couldn't have done it without you by my side all this time."

"Same with you. I've been meaning to tell you, too, that I love you. I don't do that nearly enough. But I do hope that you know that." He said that he did and loved him as well. "Before we get all sobby here, we should go and figure out what to do with the rest of our day. I'm thinking that this park by the Dairy Mart needs to be upgraded. The seats are a little too creaky for us to be sitting on them for any length of time."

"What a way to change the subject." They both laughed, and he was glad that he had this time with his brother. Brenin had always been there for him, and he hoped that he could say the same about him. They were all they had in the world besides their cousins, and he never wanted to spend a day without being around him. That was something else he was going to do: spend more time with his family. "All right. We've been playing around enough for the day. Let's get to work on some of the projects that you have piled up on your desk. I can help with them if you'd be all right with that."

They walked back to the house, talking about anything that popped into their minds. It was good to have someone to talk to all the time, and he was happy that the two of them got along so well. He'd known other families that couldn't stand to be around one another, and he hoped that never happened to the two of them. Mostly, they were humans, but they still had a few shifter friends who hadn't wanted to be around their family as well. Like his sister Margo when she'd been around.

"I was thinking about Margo this morning." He told Brenin that he'd just been thinking about her as well. "I wondered if she was dead or in prison for the rest of her life. Not that I care, so long as she's gone, but I do wonder if she's having a terrible time or not."

"I hope she's having the worst time ever. More than what she caused us." Brenin agreed, saying that he would smile once in a while, thinking about how she'd been taken down by a mere human. "I'd forgotten about that. Skye drew first blood and owned her dragon and her. That burned her toast, and we had such a good time with her after she gave her to us."

"Yeah, it was all right, but then it got to be boring." He said that it had and it hadn't taken all that long to be bored with it either. "No. I guess we're not the type of person that gets their rocks off at someone else's pain."

They had always worked well together, and today was no exception. They went through all the files on his desk in record time and had started on things that would eventually need to be gone over. Most of it was things for Ace, such as getting contracts for larger companies to come into town to help the economy. He couldn't wait for Raven to come home so that he could tell her what they'd done. He was going to start with that when he had to tell her about not being shot.

He invited his brother to have dinner with them tonight, but he declined. Spending the day with him had put him behind on the things that he needed to do. When he asked what was going on, his brother flushed a little and said that he had a date. Nothing big, she wasn't his mate, but he was going out with her to have a little fun.

"That's wonderful. I hope you have a wonderful time." He said he was sure that he would, she was part of the pack that Jenkins had. "A shifter. They're the best kind of people to date, I think. They have no expectations about how you're going to profess your undying love for them on the first date."

"Wow, that wasn't right." They both laughed, knowing that it was true. Humans saw a price tag on them when they saw where they lived and decided that they were going to be the next Mrs. Savage. Not all humans were like that, but the few that had been had soured it for the others. He was just glad that he didn't have to worry about getting a date from now on. He was as happy as he could be with Raven. She was his perfect match. "I have to get going. It was fun today, Cassian. We need to do that more often."

"You're right. We should get together for dinner once a week, just the two of us." He said he'd like that and agreed to meet up with him on Wednesday of next week for dinner. "Raven has late classes on that night, so we'll have all evening to hang out too."

After his brother left, he went to find himself a snack to hold him over until dinner. He'd heard from Raven once; she was getting things organized with the street fair and having a good time. He told her about all the work that he and Brenin had gotten done, and she was pleased with him. Cassian had already decided that the conversation with the couple would be better face-to-face. And alone in the house. He didn't want her taking him to task in public. Not that he thought she would, but there was no point in pushing her buttons when he didn't have to.

It was nearly six when she got home. She looked exhausted but happy. He told her about the couple, then told her about the gun and what Brenin had done to save him. He told her three times that he was fine, but she had to check him over for herself.

"I expected you to be upset with me." She asked him why he was all right and they'd got the people out of a bad situation. "True, but there was a gun involved. I just thought you'd be mad about that and the chances that I took."

"You did take a chance on them, but it worked out. I'm not saying that tomorrow I might rethink being mad at you—besides, don't look for trouble when there isn't any. I'm not mad at you for doing what you did, but I'm a little upset with Brenin. He could have been hurt badly as his dragon had the building come down on him. That worries me."

He didn't know if he should be jealous or not that his brother had gotten more attention than he had when it came to what happened earlier today. Smiling to himself, he thought that he was going to be forever on his toes when it came to Raven and how to predict what she was going to react to. But it would be worth it daily if she just smiled at him the way that she was now.

"You look sappy." He said that he felt sappy all of a sudden. "What are you thinking about that has you looking like you've just gotten laid? I'm sure it has nothing to do with me."

"I was thinking about how much you're going

to keep me on my toes in the future. And I find that I love that idea more than anything else." Raven rolled her eyes at him. "Seriously, I was worried all day about you being upset with me, and you're more worried about my brother and him getting hurt than you were about me. If that doesn't take your ego down, I don't know what will."

"He's alone with no one to care for him. Oh, I know that you will when he needs you, but he needs a mate. I hope he gets one soon." He told her how they were talking about that today and what Brenin had said about getting one. "Good for him. Sometimes love needs a little push in the right direction before things work out." She looked thoughtful at him. "I believe that made more sense in my head. Anyway, I'm glad that he's taking this seriously. He needs a woman in his life to pamper him. I don't think he's ever been pampered before."

"I pamper him." She just snorted at him. "I do. Of course, I make fun of him too and knock him around a bit, but I pamper his whiny ass."

"See? That's what I'm talking about. He needs someone in his life who is only for him. Like you and I are together. Someone that he can depend on and maybe even pamper her a bit, too. I can see him with a bunch of kids, too. All of them would want to be with Dad, and he'd be great at it."

"How about us? Can you see us with kids?" She

told him that she wanted some, but not right away. She really did want to get her education started right now. "I don't blame you. And whenever you're ready, I am as well. But we can still practice, can't we? I mean, it'll take an expert to create children between us."

Again, she rolled her eyes at him, and he was fine with that. For the rest of the evening, they teased one another and had a good time. They might not spend a great deal of time together right now, but when they did, it was quality time. And he couldn't have loved her any more than he would tomorrow. Christ, he really was sappy tonight.

Chapter 9

Brenin was enjoying his date with Megan. They'd gone to dinner, then a movie, and were now sipping their way through conversation at the local bar with a couple of beers. He usually didn't care for the stuff, but tonight it had felt right to have. She asked him to dance, and he did so with a light in his step that he'd not felt in a long while.

"What do you know about some of the businesses that might be coming to town? I've heard that there is a car dealership that's going to be huge and hire about fifty people." He said that was right. They were going to hire mechanics, too. "That'll be good for a lot of people. I mean, fifty jobs are better than what we have now."

Had he not worked for his brother today, he wouldn't have known anything about it. Another good reason to hang out with his brother, he thought. He could get information that he might not have been privy to. The second place he told her about was a manufacturing place that made bread.

"They ship all over the United States. And they make buns for quite a few restaurants." She asked the name, and he told her he couldn't tell her that, other than just a few hints. "That way, there aren't any rumors going around if they decide not to come here. You understand, don't you?"

"Oh yeah, I get it. I bet it has to do with the stock market, too. Something about a place expanding and then their profits might lower or rise for a bit. I understand completely." They danced a couple of slow dances and something a little more jazzy. "My mom wants me to leave the pack for a larger one. I'm not sure that I want to do that. I like the hometown atmosphere right here. She said that I'd get better opportunities if I were to go to something larger."

"There are advantages to them both, I suppose. I've lived in a much larger city than the town we live in now. And smaller ones." She said she couldn't believe there'd be something smaller than the town they both lived in. "You'd be surprised. Large towns have just as many problems as the smaller ones, but just bigger. And while I love living in the little town where everyone knows everyone, there is a lot to be said for living in one of the bigger cities, too. More nightlife for one thing. Better housing. There are opportunities, too, like your mom said. But plenty of disadvantages as well. Like here, people will help you if you need it because they know you. In the larger town, you're not going to be getting that. Nor the friendships that you have here. You grew up here, didn't you?"

"I did. And I love how you're giving me the same stories as my mom did. Vague enough to want me to go and check it out, yet scary enough that I want to stay right where I'm at." He laughed with her. "I'll have to think about it. I did go away when I went to college, but I never liked it. It was too much, too fast all the time."

"That's what I thought too. And the noise? Christ, it was on all the time, even at night." They sat down after the dance and ordered two more beers. It wouldn't affect them like it did humans, but they still had to be careful with it. But he figured that two beers each wasn't going to do that much to their systems. "Something that I did enjoy when I wanted it was the food. They have about every kind of food that you'd want anytime, too. I loved that. We don't have much of a variety around here. If you don't like pizza, you're going to be out of luck when it comes to having food delivered."

"I'm sick of pizza. It's the one food that everyone thinks of when they have a crowd of people around. My mom has it at least once a week at home, and I try to avoid that night of the week. I'd rather have a salad than some of the food we have around here." He said that he was about the same way, but he did enjoy a good sub. "The Dariy Mart has the best meatball subs if you ask me. With a bag of those kettle chips, and I'm set up."

"Don't get me started on the chips, too." They talked about food for a while, just hitting on the things that they both liked and disliked. There was a lot to be said for dating someone from where you were. You had an idea about the same things that were going on. That could be boring too, he supposed, but they were having a wonderful time and he really hated to see it end.

"I have to work in the morning." He told Megan that he did as well, but didn't want to. "I'm working for your family starting in the morning. Your cousin-in-law has me going over the books for a couple of shops downtown to see why they're struggling. I know why they're struggling. The mister takes the cash when he comes into town and drinks it all up. Mom knows both women and she said what they need instead of a hand up is a fist to the face of their husbands is what they need."

Brenin took her home, and he was home by ten. It had been a really good night, and he was hoping that they could get together soon. It wasn't like either of them was going to want more out of the relationship other than good companionship, but it was nice to be able to dress up and go out with someone that you didn't mind getting to know.

The next morning, when he got up, sleeping better than he had in a while, he decided that he was going to unpack some of the boxes that were still in his home. Mostly it was the library, and when he went into the room to start, he noticed that not only were his books on the shelf where he'd wanted them, but the boxes were broken down as well. The faeries had taken it upon themselves to do the job for him, and he couldn't have been happier. That was when he noticed that a lot of projects he'd been putting off were finished up.

The house was cleaner than when he bought it. The dust that usually told him how long he'd not moved something was gone. Even the little cobwebs that would get into the corners of the room were gone. He loved it. Going up to the room that he'd given them to live in, he knocked before entering.

He didn't know the protocol for having faeries in his home, but he thought that he could be polite. When they opened the door for him, they seemed surprised yet nice. He asked about the projects around the house and then told them what a great job they'd been doing.

"Oh, sir, it's our pleasure. We've had so much fun keeping house for you." He said he tried not to be too messy. "It wouldn't matter to us. We love being able to help you out, and the books were so pretty to put on the shelves that we decided to keep that room extra tidy in the event that you needed one of them."

"Now that they're on the shelf, I might try and read more of them. I was putting it off in favor of not having to do anything more than I had to. You've made it easier for me to get to some of the books I've been thinking of." He smiled at Brave, who seemed to be in charge of the faeries overall. "I just wanted to thank you and see if there is anything that I can do for you. I'd do just about anything."

"Can we have the scraps of yarn left over at the nursery?" He had to find out what nursery they were talking about, and it was the garden variety, not the baby one. Brenin didn't even know there was one on the land. "Oh, the other faeries have been making it work for you. There are some things that we can do magically, and we didn't think you'd mind if we made sure that it was in working order. They've planted seeds that will be ready in the fall for flowers around the house, as well as herbs for the cook you have."

"Good, yes. That's great. And so long as there is no use for the yarn, go ahead and take all you want." That seemed to excite them, and he was then worried that he should have checked out the yarn situation before agreeing that they could have it. But if he had to, how much could yarn cost? He didn't know but it would be worth it to have his shelves filled with books and the dust gone. He'd invest if he had to.

Brenin decided that he was going to have a look over the land that he'd gotten with the house. There were plenty of acers for things like greenhouses to hide, he thought with a grin. When he'd purchased the land, it came with two hundred acres. Surely there were other things around the place that he could explore.

Gathering up what he'd need to travel around the estate, he took some water bottles as well as some snacks to get him by in the event that he was gone longer than he thought. He also told his brother what he was doing in the event that something happened to him and he didn't make it back in a reasonable hour. Of course, his brother had to make fun of him.

"Yes, because I'm sure a big, bad dragon that knocks down buildings with just his tail is going to get into a situation that will have his big brother come and rescue him." He didn't get angry but did tell Cassian that he was going to get lost just because he could now. *"Just be careful. Really. You don't know what you'll run into while out and about by yourself. I'd go with you, but Raven and I have plans for the day. We're going to go shower curtain hunting. And believe it or not, I'm excited."*

"You're an idiot, is what you are." He teased him a bit more before closing the connection. Christ, he loved his family, but there were times when he didn't like them all that much. Getting going, he had everything he needed for a long walk with a couple of faeries. They'd been exploring the land before him and knew everything that was there. Apparently, there were a couple of buildings on the land, as well as the greenhouse that he was excited to be able to look into.

By noon, he'd found one of the barns that were

on his land. It was falling down and in need of being torn down the rest of the way before too much longer. He did wonder if it had anything in it, but thought that the damage had been too great to go inside. Even sending in the faeries had been scary for him, and he decided to let it fall on its own rather than waste the money on having it torn down. There wasn't anything around it that could be hurt by it falling in, so that's what he decided to do with it.

The greenhouse was up and running. It was just as Brave had said, it was filled with herbs and even a few hundred plants for the fall. He didn't know where they were going to plant all of the foliage, but if he had to, he'd give it to his cousins and brother if it came to that. He wasn't the least bit surprised to find fruit trees in the building as well. Now he knew how he was getting all the fruit for the house. They'd been growing it for him. Then there were the herbs.

"They smell so good. I can even smell the ones that Margaret has been using in the house for my meals." Brave told him that she was most pleased with the gardens that she had and was happy that they'd be there year-round, too. "I am as well. While I can cook, I don't enjoy it, but I do love to eat. And using fresh is always better than the dried stuff you can get in the store."

He watched the workers working on replanting some of the things that had been left behind by the previous owners. Using their magic, they were able to get the items replanted in no time and helped them along so that they'd live too. He loved the smell of the roses that were in the greenhouse, and that was when he saw the yarn they'd been talking about. It was used to tie up the roses to train them into certain shapes for the house. There was plenty of it to go around, and he decided that he was going to look into other colors of the stuff so that they'd have more than just green to work with. He made a note on his phone to see what he could find.

He found the second building just before he was ready to call it quits for the day. It was in much better shape than the first one, and he could easily walk into it without being nervous. There wasn't much in the barn: an old tractor with metal wheels that had seen better days. As well as a few crates of things that had been stored there and forgotten, he supposed. He figured that he'd go through them at a later date when it wasn't so hot and see what he could find. Today, he'd had enough and was headed home when Tucker contacted him.

"The couple, the Madisons, who were in the building that you knocked down, have children. They're contacting them now. I'm sure that they're going to want to talk to you and Cassian about what had happened." He said that he could do that so long as he left out the part about his dragon. *"As you might well have heard, they're going on*

about the big dragon that tried to eat them. No one is paying them any mind, but I didn't know if you know that or not."

"I didn't, but I can well imagine. *What do I say happened?"* Tucker told him just like he'd written in the report. That the building was in bad repair and that it had taken that moment to fall into itself. No point in making trouble where there is no need to have any. *"I agree with you. I'll be around if they need to talk to me, but I'm not going to be able to tell them much more than the police does."*

"Whatever is needed, I know you can handle it." He was glad for the confidence in him. *"That's all I had to tell you, and I thought that you should know about it."*

After thanking him, they closed the connection after agreeing to meet up for lunch sometime. He wondered if there could ever be a meeting between him and his family where it didn't involve food. But really didn't care, it was a good way to hang out.

~*~

Jaden was terrified that the man who'd been in the barn, her barn, was going to be making more trips out to where she was staying. It had been a nice place to stay, and she had been able to make it work for her while she was homeless.

She'd been homeless before, but never for this long. She supposed she could get a job, but that wouldn't be any fun, and she sort of liked being on her own. As she opened the next crate of things that had been left behind, she found it was full of books, too. It bothered her that the mice had gotten to them, but she didn't think about them when she was laying in the hay to sleep. That would give her the willies, and she didn't need that in her life.

The next crate held some old ornaments. She could take them to get a price for them, as she'd been doing with the other things in the barn. So far, she'd been able to get enough money for her to have a car that she needed, as well as some food that she had stored in the big barn. She looked around her new home and decided that this was one of the better places that she'd stayed in a while and might not burn it to the ground when she left. Maybe.

Jaden hadn't always been homeless. When she was about twenty, she decided that her parents had too many rules for her taste and she moved out, taking enough of their things to hock her way into an apartment. But that didn't last long. Not only had they changed the locks on the house, but they'd put a guard at the gate that wouldn't allow her to enter, no matter how much she threatened him. There were no more things that she could take out and sell after that, and she'd lost her apartment. She didn't much care for it either.

There were rules there as well. Bills to pay so that she'd have electricity on. Then there was the stupid rent that she had to pay monthly. They expected her to be on time with it as well. That was a bummer for her as she never could remember that it was due. She had better things to do with her life than work around someone else's schedule. So she'd moved out in the middle of the night, leaving all her pretty things behind.

She'd been going from place to place for the last ten years or so. Usually, it was abandoned places like buildings around town. But that hadn't worked out so well either. There was forever someone trying to get her to move on, and she didn't much care for that. So what she did to get back to them was burn the place down.

That had been what she'd been doing when the police got involved. She usually got bored with the place and would simply leave. But she missed the fire and the pretty colors that were there. So she'd been setting fire to the places she'd been lately just so she could have a show just for herself.

She was getting pretty good at it, too. By the time the fire department had arrived, the places would be too far gone for them to be able to save them. Sometimes she'd get a treat, and it would be too close to other buildings, and they'd burn too. It wasn't anything that she planned, but she loved it all the same. Looking around to see what else she could get into, she found a stack of crates that she couldn't get to. Someone had stacked them much too high for her to get them down to explore.

"Probably full of gold blocks or something." Smiling, she knew that it was going to be more of the same stuff. Useless things that probably meant the world to whoever had packed them away. "People are stupid about keeping treasures when they could just sell them and have the cash."

Jaden didn't like talking to herself, but she knew that if she wanted to have the answers that she wanted, that was the only way to get them. People just didn't understand her, and that was another reason that she spoke to herself. She understood herself better than anyone else did, and she liked it that way.

Gathering up what she could carry, she made her way into town. There was one pawn shop in the next town over, so she had to put things in her car and drive them over. The car had been sitting in a parking lot for the last year or so, and no one ever bothered it. Moving it around when she had to make trips was probably what saved her, but she didn't care so long as she could use it when she needed. And today was one of those days. The pawn shop was open for business when she got there.

"Finding more treasures, have you? Let's take a look at what you got and see what we can haggle about." She didn't care much for the man knowing her face now and would have to find someplace else to hock her wears. Things were getting too personal for her tastes, and she didn't care that she'd have to travel a bit further than before. "These are some nice pieces. With it being summer and all, I can hold onto them until fall comes up and sell them then. I'll give you a hundred bucks for all of them."

The ornaments were useless to her, so she took the money offered; instead of hocking the things she brought in, she was selling them to him. There was less money involved for her, but it wasn't like she had anything invested in the things that she brought in anyway. She rarely haggled, as he called it, because she didn't want him to remember her. Well, that was water under the bridge, she thought the saying went, and decided that this would be the last time she came in here.

Taking the cash, she decided to treat herself to some lunch. There would be enough leftover, she'd make sure of that. All she had to do was figure out where she wanted to go. There really weren't all that many choices in the town, but she could make do. It was her favorite part of having money: having food that was hot and ready for her when she wanted it.

After dining out, she decided to head back home. There was only one thing she'd kept from her former life, and that was her cell phone. Even paying the bill monthly, she had a post office box for that; she didn't mind because it afforded her some entertainment, as well as telling her what was around her so that she could get to it. The GPS was wonderful too for getting around town. She could also order things too when she had the money for it.

After getting back to the barn, she was careful not to be seen by anyone living in the house. She wished that it had stayed empty for a bit longer. Jaden was ready to move on in a little while anyway. There was only so much she could do in one town before people started asking questions. The guy at the Post Office had asked her a couple of questions today that she didn't care for. Of course, they were just friendly questions about how she was liking the weather, but she didn't like to be questioned at all.

Going to bed that night with her sleeping bag all laid out, she wasn't happy when it started to rain. It hadn't rained in a good long time, and now that it decided to do that, the water leaking in had her wishing she had picked a better place to sleep. Moving out of the way of the rain, she decided that tomorrow she was going to leave and find another place to live. There was no point in her hanging out here when she could be living in the Zanesville area. Things would be closer to her if she needed to go to Columbus, but she could also stay out of the limelight because she didn't want to be seen around as someone who might be setting the fires.

"They always blame the new faces when shit like that comes around." Giggling, she wondered what people would say about her if she were to hang out in the larger town. "Probably something about me being such a nice girl. Never bothering anyone."

She looked around when she heard a noise and couldn't see anything beyond where she was laying. The mice had been an issue since she moved in, and she hated the little suckers. Tonight, she figured that since she'd gotten into their box of books, they were going to mess with her. When she saw something like a flashlight moving around, she dug her way under the sleeping bag and waited. Whoever it was, it wouldn't bode well for her to be caught in the barn before it went up in flames.

There wasn't really any reason for her to burn the barn other than that she loved to do it. The last three places she'd stayed in had gone up too quickly for her to see much, and the fire department had been right on the spot for the second fire. Pouting to herself, she wondered if this place would go up fast or not. There was a great deal of wood that it was made of, and it was old, dried-out wood, too. She supposed she'd just have to wait and see what happened.

The light hadn't been flaring again, for which she was grateful. It might well have been lightning that she'd seen and nothing more. Going back to her original place she'd been resting; she watched as the rain came down. There really wasn't anything much for her to do other than that; her phone had long since died today, and she'd forgotten to charge it when she'd been in the car.

When she woke up, the rain had stopped, but she couldn't figure out what had awakened her. There was very little noise in the barn, other than the scratches of the mice, and she didn't think that anyone was around. Just as she was rolling over to go back to sleep, someone spoke.

"You're not supposed to be here." She didn't move for fear that someone really was in the barn with her. "You need to move on and leave Lord Savages place. You're not supposed to be here."

Sitting up when something flashed by her, she nearly screamed when the person spoke to her so close this time. More of the same stuff, she wasn't supposed to be here, and that they were trespassing.

"I'll be where I want to be, and there is nothing you can do about it." Yes, she thought, she was out of here tomorrow. And the place just might not burn to the ground either now that someone knew who she was. "You're trespassing, too, in the event that it didn't occur to you. I'm not leaving here until I'm good and ready."

Nothing more was said, but she had a feeling that they'd not left yet. There wasn't a sound around her. No more scratches on the wood, nor were there any sounds of bugs in the night. It was as if everything had gone silent in that moment. The silence scared her more than the person did because she knew it meant that they were still looking around.

Lying back down, she didn't move anymore. Knowing that her face was going to hurt tomorrow, she was so tense she didn't like whoever was in the barn. They should have just left her alone with her thoughts, as she wasn't hurting anyone. Then, as she was beginning to doze off, she saw another flash of light. She knew it wasn't lightning this time, as it had been too close to her body to have been anything but a flashlight.

"Who are you and what do you want?" She looked around to see if she could see anything, and there was no one around that she could see. "Go away before I find you."

"You don't believe in me, so you'll never find me." What the hell was that supposed to mean, she wondered. "I'm going to let Lord Savage know that someone is in his barn and they plan to set it on fire. That will have him out here in no time, even in the middle of the night. So you'd best pack up and get out before I return with him."

She started doing just that. There was no point in arguing with the person, nor did she believe that he'd be back with this Savage person. But she wasn't going to take any chances with it and gathered what few things she'd purchased for herself for her long stay. The sleeping bag was giving her trouble when she heard someone open the big doors at the bottom of the barn.

"I demand that you show yourself. I know you're in here now." She did wonder how he'd gotten here so quickly from what she supposed would have been the house, but didn't say anything as she gathered the last of her things. How she was going to get out now was anyone's guess, but she wasn't going to be hanging around too much longer if she could help it. Then she heard the ladder being used. Someone was coming up to where she was. "I've called the police. They'll be here soon. If you leave now, I'll not press charges. Trespassing is against the law, as you probably well know."

When the flashlight landed on her face, she stared at the man in front of her. It was the same one that had been in the barn earlier today. Damn it, why hadn't she left when she could have? Now, not only had she been seen in the barn that she'd been wanting to burn out, but the man had seen her face, too.

"You're not going to burn me out. I'll have you arrested if you even try. So gather up your stuff, and I'm going to let the police handle you." She wondered how he knew what she'd been planning, but she had worse problems than that. After all this time, she'd been caught, and she didn't know what to do about it.

Chapter 10

Lisa watched the people at her table. She'd been here since six this morning, and the last people at one of her tables had decided to hang around longer than lunch was being served. Damn it all to hell. The worst part was she'd not get a good tip out of them either, as they weren't ordering anything but coffee and water, which were free since they'd ordered them earlier. One of the men called her over, and she went.

"I'm sorry we're keeping you late. We've been planning this lunch for a while now and forgot about the time." She smiled and told them that was all right. She didn't have to work tonight. "That's good. If you would give us the check, we'll be on our way. The next time we come, we'll ask for you. If you don't mind."

"Not at all. Come anytime." She took the check to them after getting it out of her apron and left them to it. Asking before she left if they wanted coffee or anything more, she was surprised when they asked for water to go. Lisa didn't mind doing that at all for people, as it was hot out and she knew that bottled water was expensive. "There you go."

Back up at the cash register, Marylynn asked

her if she was going to do anything tonight, as they were short-staffed again. Not able to turn down any money that came her way, she told her that she could work if they really needed her to.

Sometimes Marylynn would have people come in, and they'd end up standing around a great deal with nothing to do. She never meant anything by it, Lisa thought that it was just hopeful business that she was counting on, rather than what was on the reservations for the night. Not that there were too many of them either.

The four men had left her a very good tip. It was more than she'd made in the last week at two hundred dollars. Excited about what she could do with the extra money, she decided that she and Davy were going to go out to eat, something that they'd not done in a long time. Davy would love it.

For as much as a seven-year-old could, she supposed. But he did love things that were different than the day-to-day. Also, when she was excited about something, he would be too. Even if it was a trip to his favorite restaurant, so long as he could have a kids' meal.

She thought that he was getting a bit too old for the kids' meal. Especially when she had to get him two extra burgers when the one in the box wasn't enough. Laughing to herself, she wished now that she had not told Marylynn that she'd work so that she could spend some time with her son. Looking at her watch, she didn't use her cell phone at work; she knew she was going to be late picking him up from daycare again. She called them to tell them she was going to be late.

"It's all right, Lisa. We had a new person start today, and he and Davy have had a wonderful time getting to know one another. His mother is going to be late as well to pick up Tommy." She hated that the daycare was so free with information, but didn't say anything. It was the only place that she could afford, and they were right on her way home from work, too. "I'll just stick around until you make it. All's fine."

"Thank you." She finished bussing her table and took the few plates that she'd left on the table to the back room. There was one person there, she supposed, waiting on her, and she tried to make his job easy. There were only four glasses, as well as a couple of odd plates. Surely it wouldn't take long for him to get them washed up and be on his way, too. She was out the door in record time and was on her way to see her little boy.

"How was your day?" Usually, she got grunts when she asked him about his day. Sometimes he'd tell her about someone throwing up on the floor or something like that. But today he was thrilled about meeting his new best friend in the whole wide world. She barely got a word in at all once he opened up about Davy Maxwell. "I'm glad you had a good time. Sounds like you were a match made in heaven."

She was only required to grunt when he asked her about her day. He'd ask some questions about her day, like did anyone leave her a giant tip, but most of the time it was just how was her day before he'd go on about something else. He was only at daycare for two hours after school, but it was enough for him to find out that Davy and he were long-lost brothers from different families. She didn't have the heart to tell him that he was the only one and that Davy was just a nice kid that he'd met.

As soon as they got home, he started on his homework. If she was going to have to go in tonight, she was going to have to wash her uniform. She only had three, and they were all three in the wash. Just as she was putting them into the dryer, Marylynn called to tell her that she didn't have to come in tonight, that she'd made a mistake on the books. Thrilled now, she told Davy they'd go wherever he wanted, and of course, it was the burger place on Maple Avenue.

They had a wonderful time, and she didn't mind spending the extra money for him to have his fill. Usually, when they went out to eat, it was because she was running behind in the day and he had to rush through his meal. Tonight, they had plenty of time, and she was happy to let him play with his toy more than he ate. Davy was a really good kid, and she loved him with all her might.

His father had been a good man, too. Daniel Manchester had been a cop in one of the larger cities around the area. One night, even though he'd not been on the clock, there had been a robbery at the store where he was. Not only was he killed when the man didn't get enough money as he thought he would, but the clerk as well as the stock boy were killed as well. It had been a struggle for her to live after that, but she had a newborn baby that needed her, and that was all she could focus on.

When they left the restaurant a bit later, she had a phone call from her mother-in-law. Janice Manchester hadn't taken the death of her only son all that well either, but since she didn't have Davy there needing her, she sort of went the opposite direction in grieving. Everything was about her son and never about his father. Even now that Davy was older and didn't much care for her cuddling him, they got along all right.

"Where have you been? I've been by your place three times, and you're not home. I just wanted to make sure that Davy had everything that he needed for the upcoming school year." Lisa rolled her eyes; it was still months away yet she had to be the first to buy him his school supplies before anyone else even had the lists that listed all the requirements they'd need. She told her that they'd gone out to dinner. "No doubt that fast food place you like."

"We went where Davy wanted to go. And if you must know, that's where we were. He had a wonderful time." She went on about chemicals in the food, and she cut her off. "What did you want besides his list for school. Which I want to point out isn't out yet."

"I just like to make sure that there are plenty of things that he'll get before anyone else takes them all. Can I talk to him?" She handed the phone off to her son and went to take her uniforms out of the dryer. They'd only talk for a few minutes before he'd be grunting at her, too, or Janice would hang up when she got bored with listening to the quietness of his side of the conversation. A conversationist he wasn't.

After he got his homework done, she checked it over and sent him to his room. She had things that she could take care of; her second job was grading papers for some of the classes at the college. It was a nice second income, and she loved doing it. Tonight, she was going over an exam on electricity, and some of the answers were pretty funny when they didn't know the correct one. Sometimes she wanted to give them extra credit for the way they explained it, but she knew that she'd be out of a job if she did that. And the money really was good.

By eleven o'clock, she was ready for bed herself. She would have to be up by five in the morning to get Davy off to school and herself at the restaurant by the time they opened. Breakfast crowds didn't pay all that much for their tips, but she knew that in order for her to work nights, she'd have to find a different sitter for Davy, as she thought he was too young to stay at home by himself.

As soon as she was in bed, she realized how really tired she was. There had been some extra people in the place today, and she'd been able to make some good tips off of them. Then there was the two hundred dollars from the four men that she loved, so she put it in the jar in the kitchen. Extra money was good for a lot of extras when there was a kid in the house.

They were doing all right, the two of them. They'd been just them for longer than she could remember some nights, but she was willing to give up something in order for him to have what he needed. She never wanted him to think that he was second in her dealings with people, and she was happy beyond words that she had him in her life. The phone ringing startled her out of her bed, and she ran to answer it.

"Ms. Manchester? This is nurse Shelby at the hospital. Your mother-in-law told us to give you a call and to tell you that she's been hurt." She asked how bad already pulling out clothing to get dressed in. "The only reason that she was brought to the hospital was because she insisted. The only thing that the medics who were first on the scene could find was that she had scraped her arm when she was going down the stairs to her place."

Lisa paused in her franticly getting dressed. "So in other words, she's just fine." The nurse laughed and said that was correct. "I see. I have to go in there, though, or there will be no being around her if I don't. But I do appreciate you telling me about her boo-boo. I just have to wake up my son, and we'll be in. But I can drive more safely now."

Getting Davy up, he was upset to be woken up in the middle of the night. He was a hard sleeper and didn't much care for getting up in the morning either. She was tempted to just drag him along in his pajamas just so Jancie could see what an uproar she caused by getting her called to see her.

She didn't have much trouble getting Davy dressed when she told him that his grandma had been hurt. This wasn't the first time that they'd been called out for something as little as a scrape. She usually did things like this when she didn't get her way and knew that she should have asked Davy about his conversation with his grandma. Something had happened, and now they were both going to pay for it by being exhausted in the morning.

They had to wait for Jancie when they got to the hospital. There hadn't been anyone in her room in a while, and they couldn't find her. Turned out she was only in the bathroom, and she was scolded for getting up without assistance. Lisa just let them talk to her that way, as she knew that asking them not to for the sake of her mother-in-law would fall on deaf ears. She usually would get the staff pissed off at her before they arrived, and it looked as if now was no different. She must have demanded something that wasn't normal for her type of — or the lack of her wounds. Whatever was going on, Lisa wasn't in the mood to deal with her tonight, and let her know that when she saw her.

"You just don't love me anymore." That was something that she'd say when she was in one of her moods, and Lisa didn't say anything. "What's wrong with you tonight? I had a fall."

"Yes, you did. And you nearly broke a nail doing it. Do you have any idea how hard it will be on Davy to have to be up tonight and go to school tomorrow? I've told you this before, you don't need to have them call me when you've only scraped your hand. They didn't even want to bring you in this time, but you insisted. Why?"

"I just needed to make sure I was all right. What would you do without me being around all the time? You'd be broke, that's where." She asked her how she figured that, since she'd never given her anything but grief. "You're mean tonight. Whatever is wrong with you?"

"It's four in the morning, and I've had to bring out my son, your grandson, so that we could make sure you weren't dying. You're going to live forever; you know that, don't you? It will be just like you to outlive me." She told her she was just being mean. That parents are never supposed to outlive their children. "It happened, Janice. I loved him too, but you have to move on before you take the risks of alienating Davy from wanting to see you. What did he say to you today that caused you to do this again?"

"He said that he was getting too big to spend the night with me. I thought that he loved that." She started crying, and it broke her heart too. "What a thing to say to his only living grandmother. He's all I have left of Daniel."

"He's getting bigger now and doesn't even like to cuddle with me anymore. It happens, and it's all right. Someday, he'll get back into it, and it'll be fine. But for now, we don't want to piss him off because we're pushing too hard or making up things to bring him to heel. He knows there's nothing wrong with you, and how do you think that makes him feel?" She asked why she'd told him. "Because he asked me if you were going to die. Would you rather I lie to him?"

"No, but you could have made up something." She said she wasn't going to do that for anyone and sat down in the chair next to the bed. "I'm sorry. I've been so lonely of late, and with you and him doing things without me, it hurts."

"I'm not going to invite you to have playtime with us. That's what I need as well. Time with Davy. If you want to have your own time with him, quit pulling him toward you so hard and let him make his own decisions. This isn't going to work."

"No, it's not. They both looked at the end of the bed where Davy was sleeping. "He's going to be hard to get up in the morning now, isn't he?"

"Yes." She wanted to say thanks to her, but she kept that to herself. "If you're all right, I'm going to take you home. Try your best not to fall down again. And if you do, call me before you do 911. We can talk together about whether an ambulance is needed and if I have to get him up out of bed to come to you."

"Yes, all right." She got the okay from a nurse to go home, and Lisa dropped her off at the house. There were no prescriptions or anything that she needed to do other than to change the band aid when it got dirty or wet, and to use caution when going up and down the stairs. Lisa didn't even go in with her, even though she wanted that.

Taking Davy home, she finally got him into bed—he was getting much too big for her to carry around anymore, and she had to wake him for the second time tonight. As soon as he was in bed, he moaned about how tired he was, and she agreed with him. If only grandma had called sooner, he told her he could have gotten some sleep. Getting into the shower when she got to her room was better than lying down for the next twenty minutes before the alarm went off. She was ready for work about two hours earlier than needed and wasn't happy about that.

~*~

Cassian found that he loved being a house husband.
He really didn't have anything to do other than to
answer questions of the staff, but he was having fun.
Today, he was going to go to the police station and
press charges against the woman who had been living
in his brother's barn, and then he was free for the day.
Brenin was on a time crunch and didn't have the time
to deal with it today.

It did bother him that she'd planned to burn his
brother's building down, but now that the police knew
what she had been doing, they were looking into fires
that were unsolved around the area. He had no doubt
that they'd be able to attach a couple of them to her
name.

"Lord Cassian, there is a call for you on the
house phone. For some reason, they called the kitchen
rather than the office one." He said he'd take it then
and made his way to the kitchen. "I'm sorry to have
disturbed you, but he said it was quite important."

"That's all right. I can tell them no on your
phone in there as well as I can on the office phone. It's
probably just a salesperson needing to hit his quota
about something, is all." He took the phone off the hook
and pressed the pause button to connect the call. The
man was talking to someone else, and it sounded like
a good argument. He didn't wait until he was done.

"You called me. Pay attention to whom you've called."

"Mr. Savage, I've had a hard time reaching you. There are a lot of you around town." He didn't bother saying anything. He knew how many Savages were around town. "Yes. Well, I've been trying to reach you as I said, and it's about the estate of your parents. Do you by chance know where your brother, Brenin Savage, is located?"

"I do." That's all he was getting until he told him what he wanted. "What about our parents' estate? That was settled some months ago."

"Yes, well, the estate did, but the insurance policies that were taken out on them were not. Were you aware that they took out policies on each other in the event something happened to them? There is also one here that I have for Margo Savage. She's deceased, too, I'm told." Again, he didn't agree nor disagree with the man. "You're a very hard person to get information from, aren't you?"

"I don't know who you are." He thought that was an explanation enough and waited for the man again. This was going to take all day if he only gave him bits and pieces of whatever he was looking for. "What about the insurance? I'm assuming that it was taken out long before now, so if you think I did it as some kind of scam, you called me, I didn't call you."

"No, no, that's not it at all. You're the only living relatives of the three of them, you and your brother." He said that he knew that. "I'm sorry. I'm not explaining this well. I have three policies that belong to you and your brother, respectively. As the only living relatives of theirs, the money comes to you two."

"I don't want it. Make the check or whatever out to my brother." He said it had to be made out to the two of them. "All right, then I'll sign it over to him. I've no need for their ill-gotten gains. I doubt that my brother will either, but that's up to him."

"As the insurance company that holds the checks, we will pay you the money, and it's up to you to do whatever you wish with the proceeds." His voice had gone hard now, and he didn't blame him. It wasn't his fault that his parents and sister had been shits to them all their life. Cassian decided that he'd go a little easier on the man. As he thought, it wasn't his fault that it put him in a bad mood whenever his parents and sister were involved in his life. He apologized to the man. "Yes, well, I'm sorry too. Not for your loss, it sounds to me like you didn't get along well with them, but I'm sorry that I've had to be the bearer of bad news for you today. But I will say it's quite a sum of money. In the millions for you both."

"It would never be enough to negate the way that they treated us. But that's not your fault either." After setting up a time that the two of them could meet with the insurance adjuster, he hung up the phone.

Calling his brother from his office, he told

him what was going on. And just like he thought, he didn't want the money either. After talking for a little while about something else, they would come back to the money and what they needed to do with it. It was Brenin who had a wonderful idea as to what the money could go for.

"Give it to Tank and Ace." He loved the idea and didn't even know all the details yet. "I know they're struggling. The house that they were living in when they were down south hasn't sold yet, and they are still paying rent on the building that they were going to use for their business. I'm sure if we told them a little about how our parents treated us—if they don't know already, they'll take the money."

"I love that." He did too. The money would go for a good cause, and their family would have hated it. They'd been born to a family of half-bred dragons, and they couldn't shift before. Their parents would have thought that they were the scum of the earth for even thinking of hanging out with them. Yes, giving them the money would be the perfect way to use the money for good and piss off his parents in the afterlife as well. Yes, he thought with a huge grin on his face, this would be the perfect way to use the money. "We'll have the checks made out to them so that there is no problem with them getting the money."

"Brilliant. I love it when a good plan is workable." They talked about how the two of them were struggling, but wouldn't take any help from any of their new family. "And I thought that we were stubborn. They're good men, but I know that they could use the money."

"I know. Did you hear that Tank has been bagging groceries at the local store? He said it's to get more information from the people that they're serving, but I know that they need the money. I wondered the other day how they were making it on the mayor's salary. Tank is being paid too, as his assistant isn't he?"

"I don't know now that you mention it. I just assumed that he was. That's on us. We should have looked into it before now." He agreed with his brother and was going to have someone look into it for them. "We'll owe him back pay, too, I would imagine. Which would help them both out, too. Christ, I can't believe that we're just now thinking about this. I guess we'll have to be more careful in the future about things like this. He's a good fit, and I don't want him to stop being mayor because we forgot to pay them."

Cassian made notes on things that he wanted to check on. First and foremost was Tank being paid. The insurance man, he didn't remember his name if he'd told him, was going to meet him tomorrow at his home, and that would be taken care of. It wouldn't take them long, he didn't think to convince Tank and Ace that they needed the money more than they did. At least he hoped it wouldn't. They were a prideful pair, and he didn't want to embarrass them either. They'd have to take the money and use it for themselves. Even if they were to just invest it in something long-term. He made a note to talk to Trevor, Kings' and Skye's son, to see what sort of investments they needed to get into.

After talking to his brother about other things that were going on in their lives, they hung up the phone. The two of them had started meeting for dinner once a week, and it had been really nice. Then on Fridays, they'd meet up with the rest of the family and have a loud dinner. Usually, it was at one of their homes, but they did occasionally meet up in a restaurant. It was more fun at home; they could be themselves when they wanted to be.

He had everything else finished for the afternoon and was starting on work that he could get done for tomorrow when his phone rang again. Picking it up, he only said 'hello' in the event that he didn't know who it was. Usually, only his family would contact him on the phone, and he wasn't sure why it wouldn't be them now.

"My name is Timothy Marshall. I'm with Burke and Burke Law Firm. We have a proposal for you regarding some businesses that would like to come to your town. We've heard that you're the one who goes over the contracts." He asked him where he'd heard that. "We're a large firm and we have contacts all over the world, sir. I assure you that we've looked into your lives quite extensively."

"Good for you." He did his own research on Burke and Burke and found that they'd been in business for only the last five years, and it looked as if the managing partners were doing some underhanded dealings as they were being looked into by the law board. Also, they only had about five lawyers that he could find on their payroll. He told the man what he'd been able to find by doing a search on the name.

"I assure you that's all a misunderstanding. We're on good terms with the law board as well as anyone else who has been investigating us over the last few months. Not all truth is in the newspaper." Cassian didn't say anything as he did a deeper search on the firm. "We have three businesses that are looking for a land deal so that they can expand their businesses. They are a part of the Fortune 500 club and have been looking to expand for the last few years with no luck."

"You send me the contracts that you have on them, and I'll go over them. That's the best I can do. Or you can just send them to me and I'll work with them. But as it stands right now, we have our own business contacts that are willing to take over some land that we've purchased with the town in mind, and have got all the paperwork started already. I'm afraid that if you don't send it over soon, they might continue to look for land deals to expand."

"I assure you that the contracts are perfectly in

line with what they need." He told him that he was sure that they were, but would still have to look them over. "I heard that you were hard to do business with. Maybe I'll take my business elsewhere."

"That's a wonderful idea. You do that." He heard the man sputtering about good deals and contracts that have everything that they need in them when he hung up the phone. Laughing to himself, he thought it was the best call he'd ever taken. Burke and Burke were going to be shit out of luck if they tried to pull the wool over his eyes about 'perfect contracts' again.

Before You Go...

HELP AN AUTHOR

write a review

THANK YOU!

Share your voice and help guide other readers to these wonderful books. Even if it's only a line or two your reviews help readers discover the author's books so they can continue creating stories that you'll love. Login to your favorite retailer and leave a review. Thank you.

AWARD WINNING, BESTSELLING AUTHOR

Kathi S. Barton is an award-winning and bestselling author known for her steamy paranormal romances and unforgettable characters. A recipient of the prestigious Pinnacle Book Achievement Award, her books have topped the charts on Amazon and All Romance eBooks, earning her a loyal global readership.

Kathi lives in Nashport, Ohio, with her husband, Paul. When she's not crafting passionate love stories set in magical worlds, she enjoys camping, exploring local auctions, and attending county fairs, where Paul showcases his artwork and pottery. Her creative spark—fueled by a muse she describes as a cross between Jimmy Stewart and Hugh Jackman—brings her stories to vivid, heartfelt life.

Paranormal romance with plenty of heat is her favorite genre, and she loves connecting with her readers. Feel free to reach out—Kathi would love to hear from you.

Email: aaronskiss@gmail.com
Blog: kathisbartonauthor.blogspot.com

www.ingramcontent.com/pod-product-compliance
Lightning Source LLC
Chambersburg PA
CBHW031955170626
46807CB00006B/2496